THE EARLY YEARS
OF BLUE FEATHER

LINGUIST, MISSIONARY, SCOUT, AND INDIAN FIGHTER

William C. Tirre

New Harbor Press

New Harbor Press
1601 Mt Rushmore Rd, Ste 3288
Rapid City, SD 57701
www.newharborpress.com

Ordering Information:
Quantity sales. Special discounts are available on quantity purchases by corporations, associations, and others. For details, contact the "Special Sales Department" at the address above.

The Early Years of Blue Feather/Tirre —1st ed.

ISBN 978-1-63357-420-5

First edition: 10 9 8 7 6 5 4 3 2 1

Contents

CHAPTER ONE

1830 Along the Missouri River

A lone woodsman was inspecting his traps for beaver along a stream that flowed into the Missouri River. The area was densely forested (near the future site of Rocheport, Missouri), and Lewis and Clark had camped here at Moniteau Creek at Manitou Bluffs in 1804. Even though he was an experienced trapper and hunter, today he was lost in his thoughts, and was not mindful of his environment. His wife, a pretty Osage woman and their ten-year-old son, were on his mind. White Dove was not happy living in Saint Louis near her husband's family, the Chouteaus, who had founded the town some decades ago in 1764. She knew that the Chouteaus cared for her, but she didn't feel fully accepted by other Saint Louisans despite the prominence of her husband's family. Their son, Blue Feather, in contrast, was a popular boy with other children and adults alike. He was handsome, athletic, smart, polite and respectful of his elders. His features were mostly European, and this probably was one more reason for his acceptance among the French citizens of the town.

The trapper's name was Gustave Chouteau. Gustave was a relative of the Chouteaus who had founded Saint Louis, but not a direct descendant. In the Chouteau family he was regarded as something of a throwback to the family's early non-genteel history in the 1700's when most of the men in the family made their living as trappers and hunters. Gustave was every bit as rugged as his voyageur ancestors and grew restless at home in the town.

The town was restless as well, as it was undergoing significant changes. It was fast becoming a city, a trade center and a major river port. Even a college had been founded in 1818, the first west of the Mississippi, which would become Saint Louis University.

On his way up the Missouri River from Saint Louis, Gustave had stopped in Boonville, which had been founded early in the 1800's by Daniel Boone's sons, Nathan and Daniel Morgan, long-time friends of the family. The Boones offered to come with Gustave on his journey, thinking it would be safer if he had company. But Gustave declined, saying that he needed some solitary time; and so, bidding adieu, he climbed back in his canoe and continued his journey.

A few days later, little did Gustave know that his solitary time was about to be interrupted. Checking his traps, he found that a cougar cub had its foot caught in an unmerciful set of metal jaws. It was bawling pitifully, and he decided to try and free it. As he bent over the wounded cub, he heard an angry growl behind him! The mother cougar had arrived and decided that Gustave was hurting her cub. He turned and saw the big cat was snarling and ready to pounce. As it seemed pointless to reason with the enraged cat, Gustave unsheathed his Bowie knife, and tried to appear bigger than he was to scare off the cat. The lion was not dissuaded from its fury and jumped on the man's shoulders and bit him savagely on the face. Prey and predator fell to the ground with the cat clenching the man's face in its powerful jaws. Gustave was still holding his Bowie knife and he stabbed the cat multiple times with all his remaining strength until finally striking a fatal blow.

After two weeks passed, wondering what had become of their friend, the Boone brothers took a canoe downstream and came upon the strange scene of a dead cougar lying on top of a dead woodsman with a badly mauled face. The cougar cub caught in the trap was also dead, having bled out from the wound on its foot. The brothers buried their friend's remains where they had found him and marked the grave with an improvised wooden cross.

Returning home in Boonsville the brothers caught a steamboat headed for Saint Louis, where they had the sad task of breaking the news of Gustave's death to White Dove and Blue Feather. At Laclede's Landing, the Boone brothers disembarked the steamboat and after asking a person on the docks for directions, they found their way to the Gustave Chouteau family home. It was a sunny day and White Dove was hanging her laundry to dry on clotheslines[1] her husband had set up in their back yard.

White Dove was singing softly to herself and was a bit startled when two men, strangers to her, stood at the gate to the picket fence and called her name.

"Excuse us Ma'am, we are looking for White Dove, wife of Gustave Chouteau."

"Yes, I am White Dove, and who are you, sirs?"

"Ma'am, we are Nathan and Daniel Morgan, sons of Daniel Boone. We were friends of Gustave."

"You *were* friends?" White Dove covered her mouth with her hands. Oh no, is Gustave dead? Was he killed by a bear?" And seeing the visitors' faces, she dropped to her knees and wailed.

At that moment, Blue Feather returned home with his hoop and stick. He quickly ran to his mother and embraced her.

"Blue Feather, your papa was so proud of you. We're sorry to tell you and your mother this, but your father Gustave was killed by a cougar at Moniteau Creek at Moniteau Bluffs. On the way to his destination, he stopped at our home for a visit. When he didn't return in seven days as we expected, we went downstream by canoe to look for him. We discovered Gustave's body lying next to a dead cougar. He had been killed by the cougar, but not before mortally wounding the cougar itself."

---

1. I cannot resist this bit of trivia. 1830 marks the entry of the word clothesline into the Merriam - Webster Dictionary (see https://www.clotheslines.com/history)

"Where is my father's body?"

"Son, we had to bury him where we found him." And in a softer voice, "Wild animals had already torn him up."

Blue Feather was stunned momentarily and then a chill ran through him as he thought of his father's violent death. Tears came to his eyes as he began to think of life without his father. He just sat on the ground holding his mother, and she holding him. Together they cried.

Passers-by quietly asked the Boone brothers what had happened. When told of Gustave's death, they crossed themselves in the manner of Roman Catholics. Two men consulted each other and decided to inform the other Chouteau families in the town. Within minutes, White Dove's sisters-in-law appeared and tried to console her. They were successful only in getting her into her home and putting her to bed.

In the weeks that followed, White Dove resolved to return to her Osage family who were farming northwest of the city, near the confluence of the Mississippi and Missouri rivers, where the Osage had been driven by the Iroquois in the 1700's. The nearest town was Florissant, less than five miles away, where Jesuit fathers from Belgium ran a seminary and school for Indian children. White Dove's father, Standing Bear, still farmed the land himself but with help of his neighbors for harvesting. He was happy to have Blue Feather living nearby in the Osage village for this way the boy could learn the Osage way of life and help with the farming and the semiannual buffalo hunt.

When White Dove arrived in the village, her parents were happy for her return. They initially wanted White Dove and her son to live with them, but White Dove wanted a home of her own. Standing Bear relented and with the help of the village men, erected a traditional Osage home for her. Like the others in the village, it was a round earthen lodge constructed from earth packed onto wooden frames. The Osage culture combined elements of both the eastern woodlands Indians and the Great

Plains Indians; thus, when the Osage went on hunting trips, they made teepees of buffalo hides. Standing Bear taught his grandson how to construct both types of dwelling.

"Grandfather, why did this village of Osage not move west with the other Osage?"

"Well, Blue Feather, this region is where the Osage first settled after being driven across the great river by the Iroquois who would not share the land with us or the Ilini, for that matter. Here we settled and learned to farm as well as continue to hunt. It is wise to have more than one source of food! We live well here. We trade with the white man, mostly the French but also with the Germans as they move into the Saint Louis area; and they let us live in our chosen way. However, the Osage who moved southwest are often in conflict with the Comanche and the Caddo nations, and they have become increasingly warlike. No, that is not the way I want to live!"

"Have most of the local Osage Indians become Christians, Grandfather?"

"More than half of us are Roman Catholics now, just as your father's family and that is another reason we have stayed in this area. There are several Black Robes in this vicinity who can give us the holy sacraments."

"Black Robes? Oh, you mean the priests."

"Yes, they are good men who stayed with us even when disease came. But they do not understand how we see God in all his creation. Perhaps our thoughts do not translate well into the French the Black Robes speak."

"Blue Feather, there are many good things that I can teach you about the Osage way of life: how to make a canoe, make a bow and arrows, build a campfire, hunt small and large game, how to prepare your kill to be cooked, how to process your animal hides, how to read sign both in the forest and on the prairie, and other things. Your mother wants you to learn all these things, and I am honored that she would have me teach them to you. But White

Dove also wants you to learn the ways of the white man, his culture, and his knowledge of important things such as your letters, ciphering, and especially how to create your 'talking leaves'."

"Talking leaves?" Blue Feather said with a quizzical expression on his face.

"Yes, you know -- these papers with your letters on them. To an old Osage man like me, they appear to be nonsensical scribblings, but a man can write these scribblings on a piece of paper in Saint Louis and send it to a friend in Westport and that friend can speak the words his friend in Saint Louis spoke as he wrote on the piece of paper. The Cherokee call them 'talking leaves'. I don't have many dealings with the Cherokee, but I admire Sequoya, because he invented a way to put the sounds of the Cherokee language into written symbols."

"In Saint Louis I learned to read and write, and to do ciphering."

"That is good, grandson. Now your mother wants you to continue your schooling."

"But we don't have a school nearby!"

"The Black Robes in Florissant have opened a school for Indian boys. Tomorrow your mother and I will take you there in the buckboard wagon and we will talk with the Black Robes about enrolling you in their school. You will live at the school with other Indian boys."

"But, Grandfather, I don't want to live apart from you and mother!"

"Blue Feather, it is decided already. I will visit you and bring you back here when the school is closed for summer and Christmas. That is the way of the white man. Schools let their boys go home during the time of the year when boys are needed at the farms of their parents."

The Black Robes will teach you more about reading, writing, ciphering, and the Catholic faith; but you will also learn agriculture, blacksmithing, and carpentry. You will get a fine education there."

Blue Feather gave a resigned sigh. He knew not to argue with his grandfather. But his heart ached when he thought of living apart from him.

It was a two-hour buckboard ride to St. Stanislaus Seminary. The physical property was underwhelming, consisting of just a few log cabin buildings that served as a chapel and classroom, a barracks for the students, a separate rectory for the priests, and a barn for the animals. The campus was on the edge of a medium sized farm run by the Jesuit fathers, which the seminarians farmed with the help of the students.

A young priest from Belgium met with Blue Feather, White Dove, and Standing Bear: "I am Father Pierre-Jean De Smet; I came to this country from Belgium. So young man, you wish to enroll in school? What is your name? I am speaking to you in English because more of the students here know English than French. Are you all comfortable with English?"

"My name is Blue Feather Chouteau, and yes we all speak English."

"The Chouteau family of Saint Louis?"

"Yes, Father. My father was Gustave Chouteau. He died two months ago in a cougar attack. My mother is White Dove and my grandfather is Standing Bear of the Osage nation."

Fr. De Smet crossed himself, "I am so sorry to hear of your loss!"

White Dove jumped in, "Gustave wanted Blue Feather to get a white man's education as he himself did years ago. He also wanted him to be taught about Jesus. We taught him what we could, but Blue Feather needs someone with more knowledge of the faith than me, and I do not have the white man's letters."

"Madame Chouteau, you have brought Blue Feather to the right school. We will teach him the doctrine of the most holy church, and teach him to read, to write, and to do arithmetic. He will also study natural philosophy and Latin."

"And agriculture, blacksmithing, and carpentry?" asked Grandfather.

"Yes, sir. He will learn these skills as part of his duties at the seminary farm.

"Blue Feather, am I right in inferring that you speak French, English, and Osage Sioux?

"Yes, Father. I speak all of these languages and can read French and English. The Osage Sioux language does not have a written form."

Fr. De Smet smiled and said, "You are quite the precocious young man, Blue Feather! If you join us here at St. Stanislaus you can learn other languages as well. I can teach you Latin, which is the language of our holy mother church and the basis for our French language; and with the other boys you will have an opportunity to learn Ioway, Sauk, and Illini because we have boys from these tribes here. I am trying to learn these languages now because I came to America from Belgium in 1823 to bring God's word and the gospel to American Indians."

Blue Feather was warming up to the idea of staying at this school, especially since Fr. De Smet appeared to be so friendly and kind, and enthusiastic about learning. The boy turned to his mother and said, "Well, Mother -- will you let me stay here with Fr. De Smet?"

White Dove smiled and looked at her father who returned her smile, "Yes, Blue Feather, you can enroll at this school."

CHAPTER TWO

Blue Feather's first week at the school went fairly smoothly. But there was one incident in which an older boy, Gray Wolf, from the Sauk nation attempted to assert his dominance over Blue Feather.

"What makes you think you Osage can enroll at this school with your superiors? The Osage are inferior to the Sauk and the Illini! Why didn't you move west with the rest of your tribe?" Then Gray Wolf pushed Blue Feather to the ground.

"Ha! You fell down like a little girl! I'll show you your place." And Gray Wolf kicked at the prone figure of Blue Feather. But before he could connect, Blue Feather caught his foot and tripped his opponent twisting him in the process. Blue Feather quickly jumped on top of Gray Wolf and struck him hard on the nose and then again on the right eye. Getting to his feet Blue Feather said, "I don't like to fight, but I will defend myself, and I will not be insulted!" Gray Wolf was up on one elbow, glaring at Blue Feather. "You were just lucky, half-breed!"

At this point one of the Jesuit priests came running up -- it was Fr. Louvain. "Blue Feather, why did you hurt this boy?" he asked, letting some anger show.

An Ioway boy, Little Bull, piped up, "But Father, Blue Feather was just defending himself. Gray Wolf started it by insulting him and pushing him to the ground."

Fr. De Smet stepped in and said, "Yes, Blue Feather was just defending himself. I was 30 yards away and observed this."

Fr. Louvain grasped the younger priest by the arm, led him aside, and said, "Well, I accept the testimony of the witnesses.

But the question remains how should we discipline these boys, because it takes two to have a fight."

Fr. De Smet said, "I think I have just the project for them, and if the Lord works for good out of this situation, the boys will reconcile their differences while learning to work together. I heard that Mother Duchense has need of some boys to white-wash the fence around her convent. I suggest that I drive them to the convent in the buckboard and return to bring them home in the evening."

Fr. Louvain was silent for a few seconds but then said, "That sounds like an excellent idea. Please proceed with your plan, Fr. De Smet."

Fr. De Smet turned to the boys who stood glaring at each other, "Boys, tomorrow morning after chapel, I want you to harness two mules to the buckboard wagon and have two lunches packed for yourselves. I'm taking you over to Mother Duchense's orphanage for Indian girls where you will whitewash the picket fence that surrounds the convent, and anything else she needs done before I return at five o'clock."

"But we will miss our lessons!" objected Blue Feather, earning a sneer from Gray Wolf.

"Not to worry, young men. After our evening meal I will give you your assignments and you can finish them by lantern light in the mess hall." Gray Wolf sighed, resigning himself to defeat.

The next morning after chapel Blue Feather and Gray Wolf immediately went to the stable to harness two fine Missouri mules to the buckboard wagon. They had with them their lunch pails which they set down in the wagon bed. Gray Wolf narrowed his eyes at Blue Feather and said, "You know, of course, because of you we're going to miss not only our lessons but also the bump hips (later evolving into lacrosse) match. So, if I ever have more trouble from you..." Then Blue Feather finished for him, "If we have trouble, it will be because you started it, Gray Wolf! I'd rather we just got along, but I'm not going to be pushed around by you or anyone else."

Their conversation was cut short by the arrival of Fr. De Smet. "OK, boys -- I want the two of you to sit in the wagon bed and hold your lunch pails because I don't want them bouncing around noisily while we drive over the bumpy roads to the orphanage. We have about a two-hour journey, so why don't we make the time fly by with a recitation of the catechism and some singing of Godly hymns?"

Gray Wolf's eyes narrowed again as he glared at Blue Feather, who just shrug his shoulders because he knew that it would not help to resist. Two hours passed and Gray Wolf was relieved to see the orphanage in the distance. The ride there had been torture for him. Then as the buckboard wagon passed through the gate, dozens of girls abandoned their games and ran up to the wagon saying, "Hello Fr. De Smet!" and other greetings. Hearing the commotion, Mother Duchense peered through the doorway of the chapel and walked over to Fr. De Smet. "Girls, give Fr. De Smet some room! How are you Fr. De Smet?"

"I have been blessed in many ways since we last met, Mother," Fr. De Smet said smiling. And you?"

"Oh, the same! And I see that the Lord is blessing us today with two young men. To work on the fence?"

"Yes, Mother. I want to introduce Gray Wolf and our new boy Blue Feather. They are at your service all day for whitewashing the fence or whatever tasks you might need them for."

"Young men, how are you with a hammer and nails? There is a part of the fence that needs repair before you begin whitewashing it."

"Mother Duchense, we have been learning carpentry from the Jesuits and we will be happy to fix your fence," said Blue Feather. "Excellent! Well then, young men, let me show you what needs to be repaired. We will pass the tool shed on the way where you can pick up everything you will need for today."

The boys had a load of tools and nails as well as some buckets of paint which they took to their work site in a wheelbarrow. The fence repair went quickly once they decided what needed to be done; and they did the work without arguing. They were aware they were being observed, not by Mother Duchense or any of her sisters, but by a gaggle of girls ranging in age from seven to thirteen years of age.

"Ain't none of these girls seen boys before?" wondered Gray Wolf aloud.

"I expect they have, but not many boys as of late. They are just as isolated as we are at St. Stanislaus. Don't turn your head just now, but that tall girl seems to be watching you in particular. She must be about thirteen years old."

"And that means she could be thinking of marriage already. Girls in some tribes marry at 13 or 14."

"Well, she sure is pretty, and healthy looking. Girls that pretty are rare in these parts."

"Now hold on just a minute! That girl might just be wanting to escape this orphanage. And I'm not ready to take on a squaw just yet. I need to learn me a skill like carpentry and find work before I marry. And heck, I'm just thirteen myself."

While the boys were in their whispered conversation, a young girl sidled up to Blue Feather. Blue Feather looked to his side and was startled to see her standing there. She smiled at him and his heart skipped a beat. She was the prettiest girl he had ever seen, even in Saint Louis.

"Sorry to startle you! I just wanted to introduce myself. My name is Winnie, which is short for Winona. What is your name?"

There were a couple of awkward seconds before Blue Feather could find his voice, "Oh, my name is Blue Feather, of the Osage nation."

"My parents were of the Shawnee nation, but now they are both dead. My father was killed by a bear, leaving me with just my mother. We followed our band west to southeast Missouri to farm. But then my mother got sick and died. After being passed around by some relatives of my parents, they heard of this orphanage and school and brought me here."

"I'm sorry to hear of your loss. Some months ago, I lost my father, who was a French American. He was killed by a cougar. My mother and I moved back to the Osage village near here. I'd be there today, but they want me to be educated as my father wished. I think that a white man's education is a good thing, because I don't think we'll be able to live out our lives in the traditional Indian way."

"Really? Isn't their room for everyone? White, Indian, and Negro?"

"The white people will keep flowing to America, from Ireland, Germany, Sweden and other European countries. You should see how Saint Louis is growing. And as more white people come to live here, the Indian people will be forced westward."

"How can the white people just force us to move?"

"Armed soldiers, many of them, will come and round up the Indian people and march them west. The other day I heard the Jesuit fathers talking about a new law, the Indian Removal Act, which will force all the tribes of the southeast -- the Choctaw, Chickasaw, Seminole, Creek and Cherokee-- to land set aside for them in an Indian Territory, southwest of Missouri. This might take years -- we might even be adults by the time all the Indians are forced into the Indian Territory -- but I think that it's bound to happen."

"Well, I want to live on a farm with a nice sturdy house built of wood. We will grow corn and have dairy cows, and lots of chickens for eggs! And my husband will be a good Christian man and I don't care if he is Indian or white, so long as he loves me."

"Wow, you've got it all figured out!"

"Yes, I do. I figure I should be married in about four or five years."

"Well, I had better concentrate on my work here. Less talk and more work!"

"Oh, listen! The noonday Angelus bells are ringing. I must stop and pray!" And the pretty girl bowed her head in prayer, her lips reciting the Catholic prayer.

Blue Feather also stopped to pray. The Angelus Bells would ring in Saint Louis too, and he was familiar with the custom.

After the last ring of the bells, Winnie opened her eyes and smiled at Blue Feather. "I've kept you from your work, and I should leave now. Can you come to the orphanage sometime to visit me?"

Blue Feather hesitated a couple of seconds then said "Yes, if I can get away on a Saturday, I'll come visit you."

"Good!" And then after a moment's hesitation, Winnie hugged Blue Feather and kissed him on the cheek.

Blue Feather stood there in shock, *what just happened?* He was quite unsure, but he smiled as he thought of Winnie.

Blue Feather worked hard at school, learning as much as he could of his school subjects. But he also tried to learn the languages of his classmates. With the help of his friend Little Bull, he became proficient at Iowa Sioux quickly, as it shared several features with his native Osage Sioux. Gray Wolf was at first a bit reluctant to help Blue Feather with the Sauk language. "Why do you want to speak Sauk? Most of us Sauk are up north in Wisconsin and Illinois."

"Gray Wolf, someday maybe I'll run a school like this for Indian boys from various tribes, and I'll want to be able to speak to their parents. Of course, we all might be speaking English by then; but I think it is a sign of respect for another tribe to speak their language. And who knows, maybe knowing each other's languages and beliefs will help us find peace."

"Peace? You really are a dreamer, Blue Feather. If anything, there's gonna be more war. Someday Indian tribes might unite long enough to realize that together they would have the strength to expel the white man. Just wait and see! We will get our revenge on the white man."

"I hope you're wrong, Gray Wolf! The Bible tells us, "Repay no one evil for evil but give thought to do what is honorable in the sight of all. If possible, so far as it depends on you, live peaceably with all.""

"Yeah, well just between you and me, I don't think the Sauk are going to stay peaceful much longer. I expect old Chief Black Hawk will finally get fed up with white man's lies and theft of Sauk land. There will be war, count on it!"

♋   ♋   ♋

Gray Wolf eventually relented and helped Blue Feather learn the Sauk language. He had come to respect Blue Feather because he was honest and genuinely interested in the well-being of all people regardless of their race or ethnicity. But he didn't think Blue Feather had the makings of a true warrior; and for that reason, they never became the best of friends.

Blue Feather continued with his quest to learn other Indian languages and actually invented a type of phonetic alphabet so that he could record the words he was learning, and sentences which demonstrated the grammar of the language. Blue Feather's invention was clearly before its time -- linguists didn't create the International Phonetic Alphabet until 1886. When Father De Smet learned of Blue Feather's invention he was astonished.

"Blue Feather, what are you writing in your notebook? I frequently see you sitting alone under this oak tree busily recording something. Are you writing stories or poems?"

"No, Fr. De Smet, not stories or poems. I am recording the words I am learning of another tribe's language and sentences that demonstrate how the speakers of that language put their words together to make sentences. This notebook is for the Sauk language. I have another notebook for the Iowa Sioux language."

"That is fascinating work, Blue Feather! You must have some reason other than intellectual curiosity that motivates this hard work!"

"Well Father, it's partly curiosity but I have another reason as well. Gray Wolf thinks I am a dreamer, but I think that peace among the Indian tribes might be possible if they understood each other's language, beliefs, and customs. And someday maybe I can open a school for Indian children where we prepare future chiefs for peace."

"That is an excellent idea, Blue Feather! And in the meantime, you might be able to help me spread the gospel to unreached Indian souls in the west! Just this past month, some Indians from the Rocky Mountains came to Saint Louis to request that we send them a "Black Robe." But we had no one to spare -- what a shame! The need is there, young man! God's Holy Spirit is changing hearts and minds."

"Blue Feather, will you kneel with me while I recite these words from Jesus Christ?

"Blessed are the poor in spirit,
for theirs is the kingdom of heaven.
Blessed are those who mourn,
for they will be comforted.
Blessed are the meek,
for they will inherit the earth.
Blessed are those who hunger and thirst for righteousness,
for they will be filled.
Blessed are the merciful,
for they will be shown mercy.
Blessed are the pure in heart,
for they will see God.
Blessed are the peacemakers,
for they will be called children of God.
Blessed are those who are persecuted because of righteousness,

for theirs is the kingdom of heaven.

Blessed are you when people insult you, persecute you and falsely say all kinds of evil against you because of me. Rejoice and be glad, because great is your reward in heaven, for in the same way they persecuted the prophets who were before you."

"Blue Feather, I think the Lord is calling you to be a peacemaker!"

Then Fr. De Smet made the sign of the cross, touched Blue Feather's shoulder and continued on his way. Blue Feather just thought *Me, a peacemaker? You can't make a living as a peacemaker, or can you?*

CHAPTER THREE

With time, Blue Feather made friends with boys from other tribes and he filled notebooks for Ioway Sioux, Potawatomi, Shawnee, Illini, as well as Sauk. The Jesuits marveled at this boy's gift for languages and thought surely it was from the Holy Spirit.

Winnie helped Blue Feather a great deal with Shawnee. On Saturdays and Sundays, they would meet at their agreed-upon place and talk for hours. The boy and girl didn't realize it at the time, but they were growing in affection and respect for each other far beyond what would be expected of children their age.

It was hard for them to part on this particular afternoon, and they lingered on past their usual time. It would be dusk before Winnie would reach her home, so Blue Feather walked with her as a precaution. Blue Feather noticed some bear scat along the trail they usually took so he directed them along another route that paralleled the Missouri River. But as they walked on and came to a copse of trees, Blue Feather noticed something sticking out of a pile of brush. As they came closer, Blue Feather realized that it was a dugout canoe. A closer look at its markings suggested that it was a Sauk canoe, and Blue Feather thought of Gray Wolf. *Could it be that this canoe belongs to Gray Wolf? Where is he planning to go?*

Early one morning before the boys were roused from their beds for chapel, Blue Feather was awakened by someone trying to sneak out of the dormitory. Waiting for the dormitory door to close, Blue Feather got out of bed and dressed quickly, and ran to catch up with the boy who was sneaking out.

A few minutes later he caught up with the boy. As he suspected, it was Gray Wolf. "Gray Wolf, it is me, Blue Feather. Where are you going?"

"Black Hawk has declared war and I am now of age as a warrior. I am 15 and I'm going upriver on the Mississippi to join my brothers to wage war on the white man."

"But Gray Wolf, what has the white man ever done to you? All of the good Fathers here at the school are white men. Haven't they treated you kindly and fairly and always acted in your best interest?"

"I'm not fighting against the Black Robes. I'm fighting against the white men, the soldiers and the farmers, who pushed us off our land."

"But that's..."

Gray Wolf put up his hand and snarled "I don't want to hear it! My mind is made up -- I'll part ways with you now."

Blue Feather looked on quietly as Gray Wolf pulled out his canoe and pushed it to the Missouri River. After he got into his canoe he looked back at Blue Feather and said, "You are a good man, Blue Feather, but half white. You don't know what it means to have the full blood of a warrior." And with that he paddled into the current of the Missouri and sped off.

Blue Feather stood on the riverbank and watched the retreating figure of Gray Wolf. His heart was heavy because he felt he had failed to be a good Christian influence for his friend; and now he might kill or be killed in this war.

Father De Smet was the first faculty member to notice that Gray Wolf was missing. "Blue Feather, do you know where Gray Wolf is?"

"Yes, Father."

"Well, would you care to share this information with me?"

Blue Feather hesitated and looked down at his moccasins, "He said he was going up north to join with his tribe in Black Hawk's war. I started to try and talk him out of it, but he would not listen to me."

"And now you are feeling bad because you think you failed him as a Christian friend?"

"Yes, Father."

"Blue Feather, Gray Wolf came to us with no prior exposure to the word of God or the people of God. None of us reached him for whatever reason; so, you are not alone in feeling this way. But we must remember the words of our savior Jesus who said, 'No one can come to Me unless the Father who sent Me draws him; and I will raise him up at the last day.' Jesus also said 'Behold, I stand at the door and knock. If anyone hears My voice and opens the door, I will come into him and dine with him, and he with Me."

"But what does this all mean, Father?"

"I think that this means God draws us to faith in Jesus, and Jesus himself comes to us. But we must open the door to him so that He might enter our heart and mind. He will not force himself on us. Perhaps that is the situation with Gray Wolf. We will need to pray for him to have a change of heart and mind. Do not despair, just keep praying; and work hard at becoming the man God would want you to become."

"Do you think, Father, I should become a priest like you?"

Father De Smet smiled, "Blue Feather, I have seen you enjoying the company of that young girl, Winnie! So, no, I don't think the priesthood is right for you. Keep in mind, that most workers in God's kingdom have not taken Holy Orders. You have talents that you can use to bring the true faith to many people. I'm thinking of the many unreached Indian tribes in the West. Perhaps someday you can go with me to minister to them. Think and pray on that, Blue Feather."

It was now 1836 and Winnie had left her orphanage and entered service to a wealthy family in Saint Louis. Their farewells were a bit tearful for Winnie, but Blue Feather tried to remain stoic. They will be reunited someday, he told her.

Blue Feather had grown tall and strong. He still didn't quite have the musculature of a man, but he was strong from hard farm work and playing "bump hips," the game that would evolve into lacrosse. As part of his general education, Fr. De Smet had been taking Blue Feather along with him on various errands. On this 28th of April, they were in Saint Louis and had just visited Saint Louis College which had been founded by the Jesuits. Saint Louis College was the first school of higher education west of the Mississippi River. Blue Feather was impressed that such a large building could be devoted to learning.

"Will they allow an Indian boy to study at this great college?"

"Most assuredly they will! And next year I think you should be ready to begin your studies."

Blue Feather nearly jumped in the air, "Would I get to live here with the white boys?"

"Yes, indeed! But I would recommend that you dress in the manner of a young white man, and not in Osage buckskins. You are as much French as you are Indian, so you would not be false to your heritage. You would just be letting your other side come to the fore."

As they neared the corner of 7th and Chestnut they heard multiple people shouting.

"Oh, good Lord! It is a mob rioting for some reason. Oh no! They have tied a young colored man to a tree and now they are piling up firewood at his feet. They plan to burn him alive!"

Fr. De Smet became overwhelmed with indignation and pity for the young man and rushed into the crowd yelling, "Release him, release him! He is a child of God, listen to him singing hymns to God! What could any man do to deserve this terrible death?"

Two rough looking characters grabbed the priest under his arms and dragged him back out of the crowd. "Shut up, you damned papist! Keep your nose out of our business. That nigger is being roasted because he killed a policeman." Then when it looked like Fr. De Smet was going to say something more, the ruffians struck him on the face and on the gut. That done they threw him hard to the ground.

When it looked like one of the ruffians was going to kick Fr. De Smet in the ribs, Blue Feather ran up to the bullies and struck the jaw of the man about to deliver the kick. It was a hard blow by anyone's standards, but especially by a 140-pound boy. The ruffian fell to the ground and was struggling to get up when his companion stepped in to grab Blue Feather by the throat. Blue Feather quickly dodged his grasp and delivered a hard blow to his assailant's gut, knocking the wind out of him. By this time, the first assailant was up on his feet and had just about reached Blue Feather when a large red-haired man stepped in and pushed the man hard to the ground. The winded man stepped in to punch the red-haired man, but his would-be victim delivered his powerful blow first and the man fell onto his companion.

"Now, will that be enough for you lads? You were abusing a man of God for his Catholic faith. Well, lads I myself, Shamus Mullanphy, am Catholic. And you won't be abusing any priests in my city!"

The two bullies looked at Mullanphy towering over them with his six-foot five inches frame and heavily muscled arms and decided to crawl away.

Shamus wiped his hands as if finishing a dirty task, and then walked over to Fr. De Smet, who was now unsteadily beginning to stand up with Blue Feather's help.

"Father, I hope you are all right. I was more than 100 feet away when I saw those two neer-do-wells picking on you. Your young man here was taking on both of them and doing a good job keeping their dirty mugs at bay. I just stepped in to assure you of safety."

"Shamus, we thank you and the Lord thanks you! We just need to find our way back to our buckboard wagon for our drive back to Florissant."

"Florissant? Why, that will take you at least five hours and you, Father, are in no shape for that ordeal. Let's fetch your wagon and the two of you can sup and stay the night at me uncle's place. He has a grand home, he does; and he will gladly take you in. In fact, he would be quite sore with me if I hadn't made the offer."

Father De Smet looked at Blue Feather and Blue Feather nodded yes; and so they accepted the offer of the red-haired giant.

The uncle's home was indeed a grand place -- a three-story brick mansion with a circular carriage drive in front. John Mullanphy (78 years old) was an Irish immigrant who became a wealthy merchant in St. Louis. Shamus was driving and he directed the wagon to the front of the house. A footman, a tall black man about 50 years old, came to the wagon and was a little surprised to see Shamus, "Oh, it is you Shamus, suh. For a second I thought dis was a delivery wagon and I was going to point you to the service entrance."

"I'm going to see if my uncle will take in these two travelers, a priest and his young companion, for the night. The priest took a beating from a couple of Protestant toughs downtown. Then I stepped in and showed them the errors of their ways."

"Your uncle is in his study, waiting for his dinner."

"Thanks, Patrick. I'll go right in and ask him."

A few seconds later, "Hello Uncle! I hope you had a good day!"

"Hello, Shamus! Yes, I did, as a matter of fact. It seems like you have a question or request -- am I right?"

"Yes, Uncle John. I brought home with me a Jesuit priest and his young charge. They were attacked by a pair of Protestant thugs downtown, and Father De Smet got the worst of it. I stepped in and laid them out, I did. But now the priest is too sore after his beating to have him drive all the way back to Florissant where he helps run a school for young Indian boys. I'd like to extend them an invitation to dinner and to stay the night."

Uncle John's eyebrows shot up and he quickly came to his feet, "A priest beaten by some toughs? That is unthinkable! Of course, invite them in at once. And if you see the maid, ask her to set two more places for dinner, besides you and myself."

Shamus popped his head into the kitchen where the maid and cook were preparing the meal, "Uncle John will be having two guests at his table tonight, ladies. A priest and a boy from his school."

At the mention of a priest and a boy from his school, Winnie's thoughts went immediately to Blue Feather. But she dismissed the idea as unlikely and went about her business.

John Mullanphy stepped to the door of his home to personally greet his guests, extending his hand to Fr. De Smet he said, "Welcome Father, I am John Mullanphy and I am pleased to open my home to you."

"Thank you, Mr. Mullanphy. I am Father Pierre-Jean De Smet, and this young man is one of my students, Blue Feather Chouteau."

"Related to the famed Chouteau family, are you?"

"Yes sir, but not a descendent of the founder of this city."

"Well, I am pleased to meet both of you. And Father, I am sorry that you were accosted by those Protestant thugs. Do you need to see a doctor? A fine physician lives just two doors down from here; and he's Catholic I should add."

"Thank you, Mr. Mullanphy. No, I will not need a physician."

"Shamus, will you show our guests where they might wash their hands, and then bring them to my study while we wait for dinner?

"Yes, Uncle John. Gentlemen, please follow me."

Afterwards Shamus led them back into the house and to the study. Fr. De Smet smiled when he saw the built-in bookshelves filled to capacity. Blue Feather looked at the contents of the room with amazement. *How could one man own so many books?* And then he saw various Indian artifacts displayed on the walls or in glass cases: peace pipes, tomahawks, mocassins, shields, lances, bows and arrows from various tribes. Blue Feather uttered only one word, "Wow!"

John Mullanphy could only chuckle, "What interests you more, young man? The library or the Indian artifacts?"

Blue Feathered stammered a bit, then with some effort said, "Both are very impressive! As a French American, I would like to be a scholar and read these books. But at the same time, as an Osage Indian, I respect the Indian way of life, which now is threatened by the advance of white settlers, and I would want to promote their welfare."

John Mullanphy smiled and said, "I see, young man, well-said! My son and I have been collecting these artifacts for years, since he was a boy. I have been fascinated with Indians since my boyhood in Ireland and am concerned for their plight as the frontier is pushed back."

At that moment the maid came to the entrance to the study. "Dinner is served!"

Then everyone started on their way to the dining room. As they passed the maid who stood pointing the way, Blue Feather was startled to see Winnie standing there. Winnie also was surprised and let out an "Oh!".

Blue Feather blinked in surprise and said, "Winnie -- You work for Mr. Mullanphy?

"Yes, for two years now! Why didn't you write me?"

Blue Feather stammered, "But I did! Perhaps I had the wrong address!"

"That is a likely story," Winnie said, looking a little miffed.

Meanwhile, John Mullanphy was looking on in amusement and said, "I see that you two young people already know each other! Winnie, you and Blue Feather may renew your acquaintance after dinner. May I suggest a walk to Chouteau's Pond? For now, let us be seated and enjoy this delightful meal that will be served!"

The dinner was unlike anything Blue Feather or Fr. De Smet, for that matter, had ever before experienced. And for the first time in his life, Blue Feather tasted apple pie! Afterwards he felt a little ashamed because he was not used to such luxuries and felt he did not deserve them.

After dinner Blue Feather spoke to Fr. De Smet about what they had witnessed that day, the lynching of the young black man. They were outside on the porch waiting for Winnie to clear the dinner table.

Patrick joined them at Fr. De Smet's invitation. "Hello Patrick, we were just discussing the horrific murder of a young black man today. I tried to stop it by appealing to the perpetrators' Christian values, but I was pulled away and beaten by a couple of thugs who apparently didn't like Catholics (papist they called me) any more than they did black people. Did you hear about the day's events?"

"Sho did Father. News like dat travels quickly among mah people. Sometimes we got to know where we shouldn't be goin, lest we want to be beat up or even killed. Dat young man stabbed and killed a constable; so little wonder the mob done dragged his self outa da jail and murder him."

"Father, dat young man was a free man, and only half black. His father was white, some planter who lives west of here. You know what? Every black man, slave or free, lives in fear of being accused of somethin by a white man. We have to jump down to the street to let a white person pass on the sidewalk. We cain't look a white man in the eyes, we have to look down, lest we be called uppity and be abused by some white man. And Lord help you if you be caught looking at a white woman! Dat's a hangin offense if day got nuthin better to do to entertain themself. And slaves, well...if da massuh aint satisfied with you, he can sell you away but keep your wife and chilluns. And if he be really mad at you, he can sell you down south, where you get worked to death or beaten to death by some white devil of a foreman. Blue Feather, you Injuns don't have it so good, yourselves. Ah hear tell dat da Army come and round you up and march you all to dat place called Injun Territory, which the guvmint says ain't good enough for white people to live but just fine for y'all."

Father De Smet responded to Patrick. "This world is not a safe place. There is little justice, and evil stalks us waiting to devour us like a hungry lion. But we can have the peace of God and live in His kingdom right now in this life."

"Where is dis kingdom? Ah'm a free man. Ah kin leave whenever ah wants to. Say, why ain't you there?"

"The kingdom of God is not of this world. We can live on this sad little world and in the kingdom of God at the same time, because God's kingdom is a spiritual one."

"Well, suh -- ah surely hopes ah kin get there before ah becomes a spirit! Scuse me now gentlemens, ah gots to tend to some business. And young man, if you take miss Winnie on a walk, you be sure to come back with her -- don't want you two to run off together!"

As Patrick left them Blue Feather asked, "Father, are people cruel everywhere -- is there no kindness, mercy, and peace anywhere?"

For a few seconds, a sad and contemplative look came over Fr. De Smet's face and then shaking his head as if to bring himself back to the present he said, "My son, as you noted, there are cruel and merciless people everywhere. It's because they don't know the joy and peace that comes from our Father in heaven. As Christians it is our duty to share the good news of Jesus Christ. But we can't expect everyone to accept the gospel. Remember the parable of the sower? It goes like this.

'A farmer went out to sow his seed. As he was scattering the seed, some fell along the path, and the birds came and ate it up. Some fell on rocky places, where it did not have much soil. It sprang up quickly, because the soil was shallow. But when the sun came up, the plants were scorched, and they withered because they had no root. Other seed fell among thorns, which grew up and choked the plants. Still other seed fell on good soil, where it produced a crop—a hundred, sixty or thirty times what was sown.'"

"I remember that story, Father! There is much rocky soil and too many thorny weeds that can prevent the seed, the good news, to take root and flourish, but that doesn't mean we should not try."

"Right, and perhaps we need to better prepare the field before sowing!"

"I think you said that people need to see Christ working in us, that we can't just preach at them."

"Yes, that is the truth, Blue Feather."

At that point Winnie walked from around the corner because she had left the mansion from the servants' entrance. She was wearing a white dress and a bluebird's feather in her hair. To Blue Feather she was breathtakingly beautiful.

"I'm ready for our stroll, Blue Feather. Let's do walk over to Chouteau's Pond. It's only two blocks south of here."

Winnie was beaming with sparkling eyes and Blue Feather could not keep himself from smiling. Father De Smet waved them on and said, "Be safe, and stay out of the shadows."

As they walked down the sidewalk their hands touched and then held fast to each other. They hardly said a word. Then reaching the pond as the sun was setting, they watched as people rowed back to the pier with their canoes and rowboats and fisherman were packing up their tackle boxes and buckets of fish getting ready to return home. Without saying a word Blue Feather took Winnie into his arms and kissed her and she returned his kiss with passion. Silently they stood there, embracing each other, not wanting the moment to end.

"Winnie, I'm going to see if Fr. De Smet will help me enroll at Saint Louis College for the next term. I probably would be the youngest student there, but probably not the dumbest. And then I will be only a few blocks away. I don't want to be separated from you any longer."

Winnie smiled and said, "I don't want to be separated from you either" and she hugged Blue Feather nestling her head against his chest.

CHAPTER FOUR

The next day Fr. De Smet and Blue Feather said their goodbyes to Mr. Mullanphy, Winnie, and Patrick. Mr. Mullanphy smiled as he shook the hands of his guests and said, "Whenever you fellows visit Saint Louis you are welcome to stay at my home. And Blue Feather, you can make that a regular habit if the Jesuits can spare you from the farm work some weekends -- I know you have your own special reason to visit us," he added with a wink.

With that Fr. De Smet and Blue Feather began their 15-mile journey back to Florissant. Along the way Blue Feather spoke of his desire to enroll at St. Louis College as soon as possible.

Fr. De Smet smiled and said "Blue Feather, I am encouraged to hear of your scholarly ambitions. But I suspect there is a young lady motivating you as well! Well, that is all right just so long as you can keep up with your studies. I know the faculty at the college and I am pretty sure they will admit you as a student. There will probably be an oral examination on Catholic theology, mathematics, and Latin; but I am confident that you will pass these with flying colors. But there is the issue of tuition. College is not free and someone must pay for your schooling. Perhaps the Society of Jesus will provide a scholarship. Also, perhaps your wealthy relatives will pay part of your expenses."

"Father, the wealthy Chouteaus are not close relatives, so they may not feel any obligation to me."

"Then let's first see what the Society of Jesus will agree to do. Your relatives might want to provide some financial help once they see the Jesuits really want you to go to college."

ლ ლ ლ

As it turned out, both the Society of Jesus and the Chouteau family came through for Blue Feather, and in September, 1836 at sixteen years and seven months, Blue Feather began his scholastic career at Saint Louis College with residence at the College.

It took Blue Feather a while to adjust to his new life. He no longer wore his buckskins but instead the standard clothing expected of a young collegian. Some evenings and weekends were spent with Winnie whose affection and devotion remained constant. John Mullanphy practically adopted Blue Feather and invited him to the mansion for dinner and once per month Fr. De Smet came to visit.

On one such visit Fr. De Smet made an interesting proposition to Blue Feather as they sat on the bank of Chouteau Pond.

"Blue Feather, how would you like to take a break from your studies this spring and accompany Fr. Louvain and me as we establish a mission to the Potawotomi Indians in Iowa Territory?"

Blue Feather sat there in stunned silence. He recalled that Fr. De Smet had mentioned an idea like this some years earlier, seeing how he, Blue Feather, was becoming an expert linguist. *But what of my studies and would Winnie feel abandoned?*

Fr. De Smet could sense the wheels turning in Blue Feather's brain and said, "Since I am now on the faculty at the College you could continue your studies in Latin and theology. We could bring the needed texts with us so long as we keep it within limits."

Blue Feather's anxiety appeared to lessen a bit but was not completely eliminated. Fr. De Smet noting his reaction said, "Of course, you are probably thinking of Winnie. Well, it would not be possible for her to accompany you on this mission. First of all, there is the matter of the potential danger from wild animals -- bears, cougars, coyotes, and wolves -- and the danger of drowning because of overturned canoes. No, this is no trip for a young woman. Second, you must be willing to be rather single-minded about your work while on this mission. You can't do that with a pretty girl vying for your attention."

"Father, I'll just have to explain this to Winnie. She loves the Lord as much as I do and she will not stand in my way. But she might feel hurt and I must prepare myself for that."

♋   ♋   ♋

Winnie understood what Blue Feather felt he had to do, but still wasn't happy.

"And what am I supposed to do for these 16 weeks that you are gone on your adventure?"

"Hey, first of all, you should not think of this trip as something I just want to do for the sake of adventure. Fr. De Smet wants me to come with him because he says he needs my skills as a translator. So I'm not going on some kind of holiday, I'm going to help spread the gospel. As for what you should do while I'm away, that's for you to choose. Here's an idea, maybe you could work on your reading and ciphering because you spoke of wanting to be a teacher of poor Indian children someday."

Winnie looked away for a couple of seconds and Blue Feather could tell she was not happy with the situation. Then she said,

"You're still thinking of opening a school for Indian boys someday, aren't you?"

"Yes, and I don't want to be the only teacher at the school."

"Well then, I guess I'll be preparing myself to be a schoolteacher!

The morning came for the Potawatomi mission party to depart for Iowa Territory. The first leg of the journey was a steamboat trip to a village by the name of Westport, Missouri. From there it was a trip by a Mackinaw boat up the Missouri River to a camp called Caldwell's Village in Iowa Territory.

When Blue feather saw the Mackinaw boats the first time he exclaimed, "Look, those boats are like wide canoes with sails!"

Fr. De Smet smiled and said, "I heard that they are called Mackinaw boats. They were first used in the Great Lakes having been invented in Mackinac on Lake Michigan. I spoke with the steamboat captain earlier and he recommended this mode of conveyance and offered to find us a riverman who can take us upstream."

"We have a lot to unload and then carry it over to whatever slip our hired Mackinac is at."

"Not to worry, Blue Feather! Again, God's providence -- the captain is a Catholic and he has offered his crew to help us carry our baggage and equipment to the Mackinaw."

Blue Feather was fascinated with the Mackinaw. It was generally shaped like a canoe but wider and longer, and in its center was a mast for a sail.

"Our destination is upstream so we will be going against the current. This is going to be a long trip" said Fr. De Smet. "But is possible if the boat can be made to tack into the wind. That means the boat must zig-zag across the wind sailing *close hauled*, which means as close as the boat can align with the direction of the wind," said Fr. De Smet.

"How did you learn so much about sailing?"

"You will recall that I sailed from Belgium to America when I was 20 years old. I learned a lot by talking with the sailors. Try to learn something from everyone you meet, young man."

"These rivermen do not rely solely on wind power, however. They also use long poles to push the boat along and sometimes men on the riverbank will pull it by means of long ropes."

The boat trip up the Missouri River took several days. Fathers De Smet and Louvain and Blue Feather arrived at Caldwell's Camp quite tired and hungry, and they still had to move their gear from the dock to the village. Fortunately, there was a small group of Potawatomi Indians who were enthused to be visited by the black robes. They asked, "Will you be staying with us for a while?"

Fr. Louvain answered "We want to establish a mission here and preach the gospel of Jesus Christ. So yes, we plan to stay for some time."

This is just what the Indians wanted to hear, and they picked up the priests' belongings and said they would carry them to the village. Blue Feather, they assumed, was a Potawatomi Indian from another village because he spoke their language. Figuring that he was a servant to the black robes, they allowed him to carry his own luggage.

Arriving in the village the priests were greeted by the village chief, Sauganash Caldwell, whose English was impeccable. When given a chance to speak Blue Feather said, "Your name means 'one who speaks English'. Are you part English?"

"Yes, I had an English Canadian father and a Potawatomi mother. And from your name, Monsieur Chouteau, I surmise that you had a French father and a Potawatomi mother."

"You are right about my father, sir, but my mother was Osage."

"Really? You speak the Potawatomi language like a native!"

"The fathers believe I have a gift for languages. I think my fluency is just the result of a lot of careful study. Anyway, I am here to help with translation."

The village they entered was a haphazard collection of cabins and tents, made of the bark of trees, buffalo skins, coarse cloth, rushes and sods, of all sizes and shapes, some supported by one pole, others having six, and with the covering stretched in all the different styles imaginable, and all scattered here and there in the greatest confusion.[2]

"This is not what I expected. This village is a disordered mess. No tribe I've heard of would want to live like this. Where is their sense of pride? Something must be drastically wrong."

"Let's go back down to the dock. I see a new boat moored there and some men are rolling barrels of something down a plank."

---

2. These are almost the exact words recorded by Fr. Pierre-Jean De Smet

As they came closer, they could see there was an exchange of goods. A pair of Potawatomi braves were trading buffalo skins, beaver pelts, and other animal skins for barrels of liquid. The white trader, a dirty, unkempt man with probably five teeth in his mouth, was apparently getting the better end of the deal, and the Indians didn't know this or seem to care.

Fr. De Smet asked the uncouth man, "Do you know how hard it is to obtain these animal skins? How much time and effort the Indian devotes to his work? What are you trading? What does the Indian get in exchange?"

"Well, lookee here! A papist preacher man come to save some savages! This is no place for you! My name is Flatnose Cogburn, the meanest riverman on the Missouri. If you know what's good for you, you'll skeedaddle right back to whar? Saint Louee? You ought not be sticking yer nose in mah business," he said while his hand went to his Bowie knife.

Before Fr. De Smet or Blue Feather could react to this foul man's threats, a tall and muscular Potawatomi brave about 30 years old stepped in between the trader and them. He brandished a tomahawk and said, "The Black Robes are here at the chief's invitation. You will not harm them, or you will surely die!"

The would-be attacker backed off and quickly climbed back onto his boat, "You ain't got no call threatening me, you..." but his voice fell to whisper, and he didn't finish his sentence.

Fr. De Smet and Blue Feather turned to their defender who said, "My name is Running Bear. My English is not too good."

Blue Feather offered in Potawatomi, "I speak your language fairly well. In fact, the Black Robes brought me on this mission to help as a translator."

"Young brave, you certainly do speak our language well, but I can tell you are not a Potawatomi. Are you a Sioux or Shawnee?"

"I am Osage, and we speak a language something like the Sioux. Can you tell me what is in the barrels the Indians paid so dearly for?"

"The white devils call it whiskey and the Indians call it firewater or whoop-up juice. It is not really whiskey. The white devils have mixed together distilled alcohol, chewing tobacco, red pepper, soap, molasses and red ink."

Blue Feather translated for Fr. De Smet who said, "That sounds terrible! It must be unhealthy, even toxic."

Through Blue Feather's translation Running Bear said, "The white devil's firewater keeps many men from taking care of their own families. These ramshackle huts and tents are the best they can do. They spend their nights drinking this horrible stuff and spend their days stumbling around the camp instead of hunting or fishing. Their children go hungry and ill-clothed."

"Somehow we must stop this whiskey trade! The Potawatomi cannot survive this assault on their culture. They need to understand God's love for them and the peace that He offers. Without Jesus they can't have peace and thrive in this life."

"The Chief knows this and that is why he invited you black robes to live among us and teach us. I learned about Jesus at a mission school as a boy back in the Shikaakwa area or place of stinky onion plants. Then our people were pushed west by white settlers who wanted the area to themselves[3]. I suppose that they remembered the massacre of white settlers at Fort Dearborn not so many years before, in 1812."

In the weeks that ensued, the Jesuit fathers began holding Sunday mass outdoors. They also began instructing interested adults in the tenets of the Roman Catholic version of Christianity in classes held before and after the celebration of the mass. Blue Feather stood with the priest and translated the service from

---

3. *Shikaakwa*, which means "striped skunk" or "smelly onion", was the original name for the area that would become Chicago. The "onion" version is probably correct because the Miami-Illinois were known for naming areas after plants that grew in or near them. It would be rare to name an area after an animal. The custom of naming an area after a food plant was practical because it provided an easy reference for gathering food.

the Latin to Potawatomi and then the homily from English to Potawatomi. In the evenings he instructed the Jesuits in the Potawatomi language. Fortunately, the Potawatomi villagers provided meals for the priests and Blue Feather. This gave Blue Feather some time each day to continue his college studies under the guidance of Fr. De Smet.

The priests were only modestly successful in converting Potawatomi adults to the Christian faith. The older generation who had been forced to leave their homes in Illinois had not experienced the love of the "white man's God" in the actions of the white settlers and were not immediately receptive. Making things worse, the alcoholism induced by the whiskey trade disrupted productivity and family life, and many people, young and old alike suffered. Blue Feather had more success teaching the children who naturally gravitated to the handsome young man of their own race. He also made time to play games with them and to practice archery with the boys.

Over their supper one day a few weeks after they had arrived and established their mission, Fathers De Smet and Louvain and Blue Feather were discussing their slow progress in sharing the gospel with the Potawatomi Indians. Then Blue Feather had an idea. "Perhaps instead of just preaching to them we should be showing the Potawatomi God's love by building better homes for them."

"Are you thinking of Osage earthen lodges?" asked Fr. Louvain.

"No, I mean log cabins, something sturdier than the wigwams and longhouses they build by tradition. There are old woods nearby that we can harvest for lumber."

"Who would build these homes? There are only three of us and we are already busy with teaching and sharing the gospel."

"If we choose one family to get a new home, we can recruit helpers who will each get a new home in turn."

Father Louvain, I think Blue Feather has a good idea. It's certainly worth a try.

In the weeks that followed, the three missionaries followed this plan and new members were added to the congregation. But nary a dent was made in the whiskey trade and drunken and hung-over Indians still stumbled around the camp. Then one day Fr. De Smet proposed a measure by which more adults could be reached through the children.

"If we secretly baptize children of good character and ask them to live out their faith through obedience and service to their parents, we might persuade more parents to come to Christ."

Fr. Louvain was disturbed by the suggestion, "Without the parents' permission? What would our superiors think of that plan?"

"Fr. Louvain, doesn't St. Matthew in his gospel say, 'But Jesus said to them: Suffer the little children, and forbid them not to come to me, for the kingdom of heaven is for such'?

Fr. Louvain stared at Fr. De Smet and then said, "Well, then I suppose we should follow the guidance of our Lord Jesus; should we not?" Thus, this next phase of their ministry began.

Meanwhile, the rivalry between the Potawatomi and the Sioux tribe across the river in Nebraska territory had developed into an enmity because the Sioux were caught hunting east of the Missouri River and the Potawatomi had been caught west of the Missouri. Both tribes felt their territory had been trespassed. Back in 1831 in the Fourth Treaty of Prairie du Chien, the Omaha had ceded their tribal lands in Iowa to the United States. This included all land east of the Missouri River, but the Sioux held on to the notion that they still had hunting rights there. Then in 1836, in another treaty with the US, the Sioux lost their remaining hunting lands in northwestern Missouri. Thus, it was easy to see why the Sioux were particularly miffed at their cross-river rivals. After several skirmishes between the tribes, Chief Sauganash entreated Fr. De Smet to help him negotiate a peace treaty.

Then one day in early August, Fr. De Smet said to Blue Feather, "It's time that you make plans to return to Saint Louis and resume your studies at the college. You might find passage to Westport on a visiting Mackinaw, or buy or make yourself a canoe, or I can buy you a horse for you to ride to Westport. From there you can find a steamboat to St. Louis. You don't have to decide this minute but think and pray on it."

Blue Feather did think and pray on the issue for a day and then told Fr. De Smet "I think I will buy a horse and ride down to Westport, and from there take a steamboat the rest of the way."

As they were concluding their conversation, Running Bear walked up. He was the brave who had stepped in when the ill-tempered whiskey trader was threatening them.

He said, "I heard you say you were returning to Westport and then Saint Louis. In a couple of days, I was planning to bring a load of furs and animal skins to Westport to sell, and if necessary, I'll continue to Saint Louis. I'm taking a buckboard wagon and I would be happy if you rode with me."

"Well, thanks! That sounds like a great idea."

CHAPTER FIVE

At daybreak two days later, Running Bear and Blue Feather loaded up the wagon with the furs and skins Running Bear had collected to sell to buyers in Westport and St. Louis, if need be. It was a substantial collection because Running Bear had resisted trading with the whiskey traders.

They traveled by day following the Missouri River. The going was slow because the paths were rather primitive and sometimes a fallen tree blocked the way and had to be moved. If they could travel 25 miles in a 10-hour day they thought they were making good time.

On their third night, they set up their camp within earshot of the river, making it relatively easy to gather water in buckets for their needs. They poured water into their canteens through moss filters. The water was still muddy, of course, but better than it had been.

Running Bear had made a campfire and had set up a shelter against the rain using the buckboard as part of the cover. They wanted to be close to the wealth of furs and hides in the wagon, just in case there were any highwaymen ready to pounce. Blue Feather put the feedbags on the horses who were still hitched to the wagon.

"This is the last of the feed we brought along for the horses," announced Blue Feather.

"Then tomorrow we'll have to wander a bit further inland to find the grasses our horses like to eat. We couldn't carry enough grain to last the trip, by any means. Say, speaking of eating, maybe we should have done this earlier, but Blue Feather, why don't you take your bow and see if you can hunt us up some meat? Maybe you'll find a raccoon or rabbit. Heck, I'd even eat a possum I am so hungry."

"Sure, I can do that!" said Blue Feather as he picked up his bow and quiver.

Blue Feather walked deep into the woods in his search for game. He came across a herd of deer, but he would have to improvise a travois to return with the carcass and then they would have to dress the deer and cut it into pieces. The sun was already setting and he didn't think they had the luxury of time, so he decided not to shoot a deer. Hoping for smaller game, he crept slowly deeper into the woods until he saw a rabbit. It was a large rabbit, as these creatures go, so it was just what he had hoped to find.

Meanwhile, Running Bear was making coffee, thinking that at least they could have something to drink with their pemmican if Blue Feather was unable to find game. Hearing someone or something climbing through the woods coming from the river, Running Bear stood up in time to see two men emerging from the darkness. One man was carrying a musket and the other a pistol.

"Hello thar!, we seen your campfire and thought we would stop and...say, ain't you that big Injun who threatened me with a tomahawk upriver a ways? Well, fancy meeting you all alone here in the woods!"

It was Flat Nose Cogburn, with a mean grin on his face. He had his pistol aimed at Running Bear, and his companion also had his musket leveled at him. "Hey, Pasquale, go see what the chief here has on his wagon; but keep your weapon aimed and ready."

"Omigosh, Flat Nose, this Injun's got a whole wagon load of mighty fine furs and hides!"

"You mean ta say he's got a whole boat load of fine furs and such, don't ya?"

Running Bear made a dive for his musket about ten feet away, but Flat Nose shot him in the back. Gasping with pain, Running Bear reached his musket and lifted it to shoot back. But Flat Nose shot him again, this time in the stomach.

"As Running Bear lay there dying, Flat Nose whined, "Well, chief, it looks like you've got your comeuppance on ya. You should never have wagged that tomahawk at me and complained about me trading firewater for furs. Now I've taken possession of your furs and you got nothing for them except two bullets!"

Pasquale called over, "Hey, Flat Nose, I told ya that Colt 1835 would come in handy. You don't have to reload between shots with a nice revolving pistol like that."

"You were right, Pasquale! Makes killing varmints pretty darn easy! Well now, let's drive that wagon over to our boat and load up our good fortune. We don't need to continue our trip upriver -- we can turn tail and return to Westport, driftin with the current."

♋   ♋   ♋

Blue Feather thought he heard two shots in quick succession, and he thought that Running Bear must have encountered a bear or cougar and fired his weapon to scare it off. *But wait, Running Bear had only a single shot musket with him, so the other shot must mean there were two men, at least, firing their weapons.*

Blue Feather stuffed his rabbit into his gunny sack and picked up his bow and quiver and began running back to the camp. When he arrived, he noticed that the wagon was gone! Where is Running Bear? Then in the dim light given by the dying embers of the campfire, he found Running Bear lying on his back. His buckskin tunic was drenched with blood from what looked like two gunshot wounds.

Blue Feather leaned over his friend and said a prayer aloud. To his surprise, Running Bear's eyes opened for two seconds, and he whispered, "Flat Nose". Then he gave up his spirit with a sigh. Blue Feather wept and continued his prayer over his dead friend's body. In his prayers he included Running Bear's wife, White Fawn, and their two children, a boy age six, and a girl age three. *What would happen to them now without a father in the family?*

Then Blue Feather realized that if Running Bear's killer was Flat Nose, then he would not have been traveling on land. His boat must be on the Missouri, so if Blue Feather went to the river, he might find the wagon and horses where Flat Nose left them.

Blue Feather gathered up his bow and quiver and ran to the river. Reaching his destination, he saw the horses and wagon standing by the riverbank munching on some of the tender green grass there. Some hundreds of yards downriver the kerosene lantern of a Mackinaw boat could be seen illuminating its sail.

Blue Feather's first impulse was to follow the river downstream to Flat Nose's destination, which was likely to be Westport. But then he reasoned it would be just his word against Flat Nose, and the authorities might not believe an Indian boy. As he drove the wagon back to the camp Blue Feather decided to return to the Potawatomi village and tell Chief Sauganash Caldwell about the murder of Running Bear and the theft of his furs and hides by Flat Nose Cogburn. Besides, White Fawn deserved to be told of her husband's death and the village elders could decide how the community might help her and her children.

Arriving at the camp, Blue Feather decided that he had to maintain his strength for the journey ahead of him, so he skinned and cooked the rabbit over the campfire as originally planned. Then, finding the shovel they had brought with them, Blue Feather buried his friend. An improvised cross marked the grave and stones covered it. Hopefully this would be enough to prevent animals from tearing apart Running Bear's corpse. Blue Feather recited the 23rd psalm and the Lord's Prayer at the grave. And then he turned in for the night. The next morning, after some coffee and pemican, Blue Feather set the horses on the return trip back to the Potawatomi village. His heart was filled with grief, not unlike the grief he felt for his father some years before.

♋ ♋ ♋

Three days later Blue Feather drove the wagon into the Potawatomi village. By good fortune, the first person he encountered was Father De Smet, who was surprised to see Blue Feather.

"This is not good news that you have returned here alone!" said Father De Smet.

"No, Father -- I bring sad news. Let's go someplace where I can relate my story first to you in private."

Finding that place, Blue Feather related the whole tragic story to Father De Smet.

"We must go and tell White Fawn the sad news, and then also Chief Sauganash. He will probably want to assemble his council of elders."

Father De Smet and Blue Feather then went to the teepee of Sister Hope, a Potawatomi widow who had dedicated her life to Christ. The men told Sister Hope the news and she decided to drop everything and go with them to talk to White Fawn and help comfort her.

Leaving Sister Hope with a sobbing White Fawn, Father De Smet and Blue Feather went to the teepee of Chief Sauganash. When Blue Feather finished his testimony, Chief Sauganash called for a council of the village elders; and Blue Feather repeated his testimony to this council.

A war chief known as Soaring Eagle was the first to question Blue Feather, "Young man, I believe your story because you have always spoken to us the truth which we believe comes from your God. You say that Flat Nose killed Running Bear three nights ago and then most likely turned his boat downriver? Why do you say that son?"

"Because there was no traffic on the river that night except for one boat which I could see a few hundred yards south of where the horses and wagon were abandoned. I didn't actually see much of the boat, but its sail was illuminated by the glow of a kerosene lamp."

"How many men did this Flat Nose have with him?"

"Chief Soaring Eagle, Flat Nose always traveled with his partner, Pasquale, and no one else."

"And you say that he would be going to Westport to sell his stolen goods?"

"That is the first port on the Missouri where fur traders congregate, sir."

With fire in his eyes, Chief Soaring Eagle stood up and said, "Then we must assemble a war party to go after Flat Nose and seek our revenge! Who will come with me?"

Chief Sauganash sighed and said, "I will lead this mission as the tribal chief. We must not simply set out to kill Flat Nose and Pasquale. We must find them and arrest them and bring them to the white man for them to be prosecuted under their law. Otherwise, some white men might seek revenge against our people."

War Chief Soaring Eagle grunted his assent and said, "Elders, choose four brave warriors to come with us to Westport. We will leave tomorrow at first light and travel to Westport by canoe."

Father De Smet caught Chief Sauganash's attention and said, "Blue Feather will write out his testimony and I will add my affidavit testifying to its truth. You will need this paper when you go to the legal authorities in Westport."

"That is an excellent idea, Father. I will take this letter with me."

☙ ☙ ☙

At first light, the warriors led by Chief Sauganash and War Chief Soaring Eagle, began their journey downstream to Westport. They were armed with bows and arrows, tomahawks, and knives. Although Chief Sauganash wanted to capture Flat Nose and Pasquale alive and bring them to white justice, the warriors had a different plan in mind. The two white men, if caught, will die trying to escape. Thus, Running Bear would be avenged.

Father De Smet and Blue Feather discussed with White Fawn different options she might have for her future as a widow with children.

"I have no kin and my husband had no kin in this village. No one is obligated to help me," White Fawn said with tears in her eyes.

"White Fawn, my people, the Osage of Missouri, would have a place for you in their village. My mother would welcome you and your children into her home for she is alone now; and my grandfather would be pleased to teach your boy the ways of a hunter and farmer. So, you are welcome to come with me in the wagon to my grandfather's village near St. Louis."

White Fawn looked pleased, and with a smile said, "Your offer is most generous. You are a sweet and noble young man. We will come with you. Father De Smet, is this not like Naomi and Ruth? Your people shall be my people, and your God shall be my God?"

Father De Smet smiled and said, "I see that you were paying attention in our religious instruction! Yes, this is much like that situation."

"Then can we leave tomorrow morning? I have very little to pack."

"Well, yes we can leave tomorrow morning!"

White Fawn stood up and said, "I will go pack now and tell my children of the great adventure they are going to have."

Father De Smet had an ill-formed thought, a vague impression that White Fawn might have had more in mind by her analogy to Naomi and Ruth; but he dismissed it as nonsense.

The next morning at first light, White Fawn and her children had the buckboard wagon packed with clothing, sleeping mats, cooking utensils, pots and pans, earthen dishes, and a disassembled teepee. Women came from the village with gifts of food and blankets, hugging White Fawn and her children. Some of the women gave Blue Feather a knowing smile. But Blue Feather was oblivious to the signals that something was happening of which he was unaware.

White Fawn introduced Blue Feather to Running Bear's wolf-dog, named Protecteur, who took an immediate liking to him. The dog would be coming with them, White Fawn explained, but trotting alongside them. He would feed himself with squirrels and rabbits unaware of the danger he posed.

They traveled about twenty five miles that first day, stopping early enough to have light to set up the teepee, and to find dry wood for a campfire.

When it reached the time for the children to be put to bed, White Fawn did so with her usual routine, which included a family prayer. Blue Feather was invitcd to pray with them.

Shortly after that, Blue Feather found his bed roll and announced that he would sleep under the wagon. But White Fawn would not hear of it, "I would feel a lot safer if you slept in the teepee with us, she said plaintively. So, in the end, Blue Feather put his bedroll down opposite of White Fawn, and promptly fell asleep.

Blue Feather had fallen asleep and was dreaming of Winnie. They were in love but true to their faith, they were both still virgins. Quietly White Fawn sat up and removed her clothing. Then she crawled over to Blue Feather's blanket and lay down close to him. Blue Feather rolled over on his side to face White Fawn, still asleep, but now acting out his dream. He gently extended his arm over her and touched her bare flesh. Soon White Fawn fell asleep and remained asleep for a couple of hours. Then waking, she gently extracted herself from Blue Feather's embrace and returned to her own blanket. She woke up first and went about the business of making a fire and making some coffee. He had not asked her to do this, but she thought that he probably drank coffee since he was a white man as well as an Indian.

"How did you sleep, Blue Feather?

"I slept well but wow, did I ever have such a realistic dream."

"Oh, what was your dream about?"

"Uh, I don't think I want to say anything about it. It's kind of private."

White Fawn, thinking of how Blue Feather had lovingly held her body during the night, was a little disappointed he had not realized he had experienced something more than a realistic dream, said, "Well, then let's just eat this pemmican and berries I brought with us. The coffee should be ready now."

"Thank you very much, White Fawn."

White Fawn thought, *You are welcome, Blue Feather. I enjoyed it too.*

♋   ♋   ♋

There was little excitement that day until a mother black bear and her three cubs ambled out of the forest into the path of the wagon. The horses were startled and screamed a bit. But the mother bear was not interested in any horse flesh, nor was she interested in the humans she had happened to encounter. She was mostly concerned with one of her cubs who had decided to climb a tree, one that was little more than a sapling. Unfortunately, the cub had climbed high and far out enough to bend the sapling over so that he was hanging directly over the horses. Falling on his back onto one of the horses, he was promptly bucked off and landed awkwardly on the ground. Mother bear stood on her hind legs and sniffed the air and growled softly. The horses' fears were rekindled.

Protecteur had been lagging behind the wagon after being distracted by a squirrel in the woods. Returning now with a squirrel in his mouth he quickly sized up the situation and came running and barking. The cubs quickly scrambled behind their mother and she and the cubs retreated hastily in the woods. Protecteur stood barking on the edge of the woods until the bears were out of sight.

Blue Feather glanced at White Fawn and then at the large dog, "Good dog, Protecteur! You certainly lived up to your name!"

White Fawn smiled. She was glad the dog had returned in time to drive away the bears. She felt safe with Protecteur and with Blue Feather and rested her head against his shoulder for a moment.

Blue Feather was puzzled a bit with the gesture but didn't let it trouble him much.

That evening they stopped again before dusk and set up the teepee. Blue Feather took up his bow and quiver after they had set up the teepee and said, "White Fawn, I'm going to hunt for some game so we can eat some fresh meat tonight. Please hold onto Protecteur so that he stays with you. You should not be bothered by any wild animal with him guarding you."

"OK, Blue Feather! Good luck!"

It didn't take long before he encountered a large raccoon which he killed as it scrambled up a tree. Throwing it into his sack he headed back to their camp. He was about 100 yards away when he heard White Fawn scream and then Protecteur barking. A large bobcat had wandered to the edge of the camp. When Protecteur spotted him, he lunged at the 50-pound cat. The cat decided to cut his losses and ran for the trees. He quickly selected one and scrambled deftly out of reach.

White Fawn had gathered her children and retreated into the teepee. "Oh, I am so glad you returned, Blue Feather!" she said and ran to hug him.

Blue Feather thought she was making a bigger commotion about this than was necessary, and he gently removed himself from her embrace. "I knew that you would be safe here alone with Protecteur. Now, while we still have some light let's build ourselves a good campfire, skin this raccoon and cook him up for supper."

"Oh, you are all business, aren't you? Just like a man"! Then she kissed him on the cheek, grabbed the game sack and set out to make supper.

Blue Feather watched White Fawn as she prepared the raccoon for cooking, and at the same time keeping an eye on her small children. Protecteur muzzled the little girl back toward her mother if she looked like she was going to totter off. The boy's attention was all on his play, which appeared to be a tiny model teepee made with sticks and leaves serving as buffalo hides. Blue Feather was building up the fire, but he couldn't help looking at White Fawn, who was certainly attractive. She was still thin but had ample breasts which bounced while she worked.

Oh my gosh! Why am I thinking about her this way? Is this what Father De Smet said is lust? Blue Feather shook his head and tried to redirect his gaze, but then White Fawn looked up and saw him watching her and smiled at him.

They passed the dinner with almost no conversation and then wordlessly cleaned up after themselves. White Fawn tended to the children, getting them ready for bed, and then asked, "Could you tell the children a story about Jesus?"

Blue Feather said, "Of course I will!" Then he proceeded to tell the children the story about how Jesus forbade his disciples from preventing mothers from bringing their children to him. Blue Feather related the story mostly in his own words.

"One day after Jesus had taught the people about God's love and healed the many sick persons, some parents brought their children to Jesus so he could lay his hands on them and pray for them. But the disciples scolded the parents for bothering him. But Jesus said, 'Let the little children come to me. Don't stop them! For the Kingdom of Heaven belongs to those who are like these children.' And he took a little boy and his sister and held them on his lap. And he placed his hands on their heads and blessed them before he left."

White Fawn smiled as she watched Blue Feather with her children. She thought, *Oh, he will make such a good father for them!* And she felt even more attraction to him.

That night she once again asked Blue Feather to sleep in the teepee with them. And once again, when he appeared to be sound asleep, she took off her dress and lay down next to him. But unlike last time, she fell asleep and didn't leave his side. In the morning, they woke up almost simultaneously. Blue Feather woke up and realized that he had a naked woman lying next to him. She opened her eyes and smiled at him.

"Oh my gosh, what are you doing here? Where are your clothes? Were you here all night?"

"Good morning, Blue Feather! That was very nice last night."

"Did we, I mean did anything happen? I am so sorry, White Fawn."

"You don't have anything to be sorry about. I enjoyed being with you."

"But White Fawn, somehow I gave you the wrong impression."

"Blue Feather, we are like Boaz and Ruth in the Bible. You said as much, yourself. You are taking me, a widow, to live in your mother's house among your own people. And I shall be your wife."

"Oh, White Fawn, I can't marry you. I told you about Winnie, the girl I love. And I'm not even 18 yet, and I must finish college."

"I am only 21 and Winnie can be your second wife, I am willing to share you with her. Many tribes allow a brave to have more than one wife; and in the Bible Jacob had both Lea and Rachel, and David had many wives. God didn't disapprove."

"But I want only one wife."

"Are you saying that you don't love me? Because I don't be-lieve you. I know how you look at me."

"White Fawn, I can't deny that I am attracted to you. You are a beautiful young woman. But my heart isn't big enough to love two women."

White Fawn looked hurt and was tearing up, "Then you should not have lured me into taking this journey with you!"

"I was offering you an opportunity to live among the Osage who are quite prosperous compared to the Potawatomi. My mother will love you and help you and your children get on your feet again. And I believe, with all my heart, that some Osage brave will want to marry you. But you will have to give it some time. If it is in God's will, it will happen." The rest of the trip was passed mostly in silence. Blue Feather still told the children Bible stories at bedtime, which both they and White Fawn appreciated. At night, they continued to sleep in the same teepee, but White Fawn did not disrobe.

Ꮑ   Ꮑ   Ꮑ

On the fifteenth day of their journey they were approach-ing Saint Charles, Missouri when they encountered a covered wagon led by a team of four mules. From a longways off, Blue Feather could see that its driver was a tall young man, possi-bly with red hair, mostly covered by a slouch hat. As they drew closer, Blue Feather could see that it was his old friend, Shamus Mullanphy. The two wagons were about 30 yards separated when Blue Feather began waving his coonskin cap and yelling, "Hey Shamus, Shamus Mullanphy!"

Shamus had been absent-mindedly watching the business ends of his mules when he thought he heard his name called. He looked up with a start and saw a young man waving his coonskin cap at him. Next to him was a very attractive Indian woman, and then as he continued to watch, two little faces appeared behind the seat.

Did that young lad marry himself a widow with two small children? Well, I must investigate this, I should. He would not admit it to himself, but he felt a twinge of envy. Here he was at 27 with no woman at his side.

The two wagons pulled over to the side of the rough wagon trail and the two young men caught up with each other.

"Hello, Blue Feather! I heard from me uncle that you had traveled west with Father De Smet to start an Indian mission. Are ye back now, and with a bride and children?"

"What? No, not man and wife. My travel companions are White Fawn and her children, Patrick and Fiona. White Fawn has become like my sister, and she is coming with me to live with my mother and the Osage tribe. She is the widow of a good friend."

"Widow, you say? Well, my deepest condolences, White Fawn. Did I hear your children's names correctly, Patrick and Fiona? Those are good Irish names, they are!"

"My mother, Kayleigh, was Irish. So, I honor her people with these names," White Fawn said with a pretty smile. "My mother had red hair like yours! Are you Irish yourself, Shamus?"

"I most certainly am, White Fawn. I came here from Ireland less than a year ago. I was a farm lad, having grown up on my parents' farm. City life is not for me. That is why I have left Saint Louis -- oh, what a dirty and foul-smelling place -- to start up me own farm!"

White Fawn spoke up, "Listen, it's late in the afternoon and not much daylight remains. Why not camp together tonight, right here?"

"That would be a splendid idea, miss. When I left me uncle's place this morning, the cooks, including your little Winnie, Blue Feather, loaded me up with a fine stew bone and vegetables. All we need to do is filter and boil some water!"

Shamus had jumped down from his wagon to walk over to White Fawn's side and had taken her hand in his, and she smiled. Just then, Protecteur walked over and sniffed Shamus's rear end, as some dogs are wont to do. It startled Shamus a bit when he turned around to see who or what had become a little too familiar with him.

"Oh, holy mother of God, has this wolf been following you?" Blue Feather laughed and said, "Oh, that is White Fawn's wolf dog. He goes by the name of Protecteur."

"He's friendly, is he?"

"Yes, just speak softly and sweetly to him and he'll let you pet him...usually," said White Fawn.

"Usually, you say? Well, I suppose it's worth a try. Blue Feather, if he goes for my family jewels, you'll pull him off, won't you?"

"Sure thing. Of course, he might decide to go for your throat."

"Oh, now you're just having some fun at my expense!"

Blue Feather and White Fawn just laughed.

♋   ♋   ♋

The camp was a fun and lively place that evening. At one point, Shamus excused himself and walked over to his covered wagon. He came back to the campfire holding a guitar. "I thought it would be nice to hear some Irish folk songs, especially in honor of this Irish lass, White Fawn."

And he sang and accompanied himself on the guitar:

Red is the rose that in yonder garden grows
Fair is the lily of the valley
Clear is the water that flows in yonder stream
and my love, it is fairer than any.
Over the Mountain, and down into the Glen
To a little Irish Cot in the Valley,
Where the Thrush and the Linnett Sing their

Dittees and their songs and my love leaning over the half door.
Down by the seashore, on a cool summer's eve,
with the wind blowing over the heather,
Oh, the moon it shone fair, through her threads of golden hair and
she vowed she would love me forever.
It's not for parting with my sister Kate,
It's not for the loss of my Mother....
It's all for the loss of my bonnie Irish lass
That I'm leaving my homeland forever.

When he finished, White Fawn said, "That was lovely. And I have to say, it seems that those words have some real personal meaning for you."

"Aye lass, they do."

"Did you lose the love of your life in Ireland? I'm so sorry if that is so. I know something of that sorrow myself."

"Aye, lass I did, and I crossed the great ocean for a fresh start here in America."

"And someday you will find love again in this great country."

"You know? I have more faith now than ever that I will be so blessed."

At bedtime Blue Feather told his usual Bible story to the children, and Shamus played and sang "Amazing Grace." Shamus had a fine singing voice and White Fawn and her children listened to him with rapt attention.

Blue Feather took his bedroll and spread it under the buckboard wagon because he did not want to give Shamus the wrong impression by sleeping in White Fawn's teepee. A few yards away, Shamus spread out his bedroll under his covered wagon.

It was a couple of hours later when Shamus felt something or someone lying next to him. It was White Fawn and she had snuggled up to him. Shamus awoke and thought that he must be dreaming and said so softly to himself. White Fawn raised herself on one elbow and said,

"No, you are not dreaming. I just want you to know that I can help you forget that Irish girl. I can go with you and be your bride. Does that interest you at all?"

Shamus stammered a bit and when he found his voice he said,

"Yes, it does interest me, me darling. But would you be willing to be a farmer's wife and have his children? I don't expect it to be an easy life, just an honest life of hard work."

"I am willing, where you go, I will go. Your people will become my people, and your God will become my God." Then she kissed him and slinked back to her teepee.

Shamus sat up and bumped his head on the bottom of his wagon. "Ow! Holy mother of God, but does that young lady make up her mind fast. Good Lord, if this is not in accordance with your will, please let me know soon." And with that he fell back asleep.

The next morning White Fawn made coffee and fried up some bacon that Shamus had brought with him. As they ate their breakfast, White Fawn announced, "I have decided to go with Shamus to be his wife and help him start his farm. Blue Feather, I appreciate your offer to stay with the Osage, but Shamus and I have fallen in love. We will marry and I will have his children."

Blue Feather sat there in stunned silence for a few seconds and looked over to Shamus, who said, "We decided this late last night. I will be a good husband to White Fawn and father to her children, and she will be a fine wife, just what this Irish soul needs."

Several thoughts whirled through Blue Feather's mind competing for attention. *Is this wise for either one of them or is it too hasty? But who am I to advise them? Clearly, White Fawn has been thinking of remarriage since before we started our journey.*

"Well, I am happy for both of you! Shamus, do you need to buy land for your farm?"

"The saints be praised! My uncle bought the farm for me. I just need to build us a log cabin. I have the mules for the plow already and farm implements in the wagon."

"Do you have a musket and a bowie knife? And an axe and hammer, and other tools for carpentry?"

"Aye, lad. I have all these things. And now with White Fawn, I have everything I will ever need! The farm is near a village called St. Peter's, which started its life as a Jesuit mission. So, we'll even have a church and access to the sacraments."

"Well, then it seems the four of you will be going in a different direction than I am going, so we'll part company soon. I guess the thing for me to do is to go into Saint Charles and catch a riverboat down to St. Louis."

"Blue Feather me boy, we'll take you to the landing where you can book passage down to St. Louis. Do you have enough money for a ticket?"

"Yes, I have the money."

As they continued their wagon journey, White Fawn now sitting next to Shamus, Blue Feather felt a twinge of envy as he realized that beautiful girl could have been his. But then he remembered Winnie and her undying devotion to him and their unspoken promises. She was still the most beautiful girl he had ever known, wasn't she? And after all, he wasn't ready to marry and become a father. With a sigh, mostly of relief, Blue Feather smiled to himself and decided to press on. College awaited and so did the girl he truly loved.

After unloading his sack of books and clothes from the buckboard, Blue Feather said his goodbyes. White Fawn hugged him and drew him close to kiss him on the cheek and whispered, "Don't dwell on what could have been, think instead of the future that lies ahead of you." Then for all to hear, "I am pleased you think of me as your sister. My children will think of you as their uncle. Will you come to visit us?"

"I will, I promise! My best wishes for all of you!"

Traveling with the current, the steamboat ride was less than two hours long. Arriving in the late afternoon, Blue Feather immediately set off on foot for the Mullanphy mansion, about three miles from the boat landing.

As he approached the mansion, Patrick noticed him and came running saying loudly, "Oh, if it ain't Mistuh Blue Feather! You sho is a sight for sore eyes! Let me helps you with dem bags. Oh, miss Winnie will be so happy to see you after all dese weeks! She be out fetchin things at Soulard Market right now, but she return soon. Meanwhile, let's show you to old Massah Mullanphy. He's gonna want to put you up in the guest room."

Patrick led Blue Feather into the mansion and directly to Mr. Mullanphy's study. The old man looked up as Patrick announced himself and then said, "Massuh Mullanphy, look who has come home to roost" and then he stepped aside to show Blue Feather.

Mr. Mullanphy smiled broadly and rose from his chair saying, "Blue Feather, my boy, it is good to see you son, safe and sound!"

"It's good to be back, sir! I brought something back for you from the Potawatomi village."

"Really? Well, let's see what it is!"

Blue Feather reached into the cloth bag he was carrying and pulled out a peace pipe. "This is a genuine Potawatomi peace pipe for your collection."

Mr. Mullanphy was thrilled to receive it. "Why, look at this intricate carving of a buffalo head for the bowl! Blue Feather, this pipe will have a special place in my collection. Thank you so much!"

"You are welcome, sir!"

"Patrick, will you tell the cook that we will set a place for Blue Feather at the dining table this evening? And a place for his sweetheart, Winnie, as well.

Patrick's eyebrows raised a bit at this blurring of the line between master and servant, but he simply said, "Ah will go do that now, suh."

"Blue Feather, you still have the aroma of the wilderness about you! You should freshen up in the bath house before Winnie returns. You know where it is, right?"

"Yes, sir."

"Do you have any clean clothes?"

Blue Feather looked a bit embarrassed and said he didn't.

"That will not be a problem. I will have Patrick bring some of my son's left-behind clothing to the bath house. He's away in England right now."

A few minutes later, washed and wearing clean clothes, Blue Feather sat on a wooden chair in the root cellar, where Winnie would appear with her food items. When Winnie arrived with her shopping basket, she was so absorbed into her task of putting items away, that she didn't notice Blue Feather sitting there.

Winnie came into the root cellar and set her basket down on the table. Then sensing something, she looked at Blue Feather for a full second and then shrieked.

"Oh, Blue Feather, you nearly scared the living daylights out of me! And then she began to cry. Blue Feather stood up and hugged her fiercely, kissing her face, and then the two of them kissed passionately.

Coming up for air, Winnie said, "I don't want us to be apart ever again!"

"I don't either if it can be avoided. God only knows!"

"Yes, only God knows, but we can pray that we're always together."

When dinner was served by the cook and Winnie, who had insisted on helping, Winnie was wearing one of her pretty dresses and Blue Feather was wearing some hand-me-down clothing from the younger Mr. Mullanphy. Blue Feather had told the story of the Jesuit mission at the Potawatomi village, of the whiskey trade that was devastating the population there, and the spotty reception the gospel had received there. When Winnie excused herself to help the cook clear the table and wash the dishes, Mr.

Mullanphy suggested that he and Blue Feather retire to his study for cigars.

When they were alone, Blue Feather told Mr. Mullanphy about the unscrupulous whiskey trader, Flat Nose Cogburn and his henchman, Pasquale, and how Running Bear put himself between the low-lifes and Father De Smet when Flat Nose threatened Fr. De Smet with a Bowie knife. And then he related the story of Running Bear's murder, and how Running Bear had named his killer with his dying breath.

"I returned to the Potawatomi village to report what had happened. It seemed only fair and right for me to do this, as Running Bear left a wife and two small children. Father De Smet and I met with the chief and the war chief, and the war chief left with some of his braves to pursue Flat Nose and Pasquale to Westport. The chief Saganaush, who is half white, told them only to arrest the killers and turn them over to the authorities."

"Well, my boy, I would expect that the Potawatomi applied their own law and exacted revenge."

Blue Feather hesitated a second but then said, "Sir, you are probably right. I was hoping that the culprits would be brought to justice in the white man's court of law, but it seems that the courts would have only my testimony, and what am I, but an Indian boy. No one is going to believe me."

"The world being what it is, you are probably right, young man. It is hard for justice to prevail in this life."

Blue Feather and Winnie went for a stroll to Chouteau's Pond, with Winnie pressing close to him as they walked. They sat at a park bench looking over the canoeists and other boaters on the small lake.

"I studied hard while you were gone, Blue Feather. But now I don't think I want to be a teacher. I'm thinking instead of becoming a nurse and help mothers with birthing babies. There is school in Philadelphia that trains girls on how to do this and I'm hoping for a similar school to open in Saint Louis. In the meantime,

Dr. Caldwell, who lives down the street, gave me a copy of the nurse's guide. This is a book containing instructions to females who wish to 'engage in the important business of nursing mother and child in the lying-in chamber'. I memorized that last part from the title."

Blue Feather was silent for a few seconds and then said, "I think this is a good decision. Nurse/midwives will be needed anywhere we might go. Perhaps Dr. Caldwell can find an experienced midwife to mentor you. I'm supposing that you will be learning about first aid and taking care of the sick as well?"

"Yes, I am already reading books on those subjects" Winnie said with a smile.

"That's great" said Blue Feather and they hugged and kissed.

CHAPTER SIX

B lue Feather returned to college and took courses in mathematics, theology, Latin, Greek and Hebrew. He was recognized as a talented and hard-working student, and he won the admiration of both his fellow students and faculty.

Then in 1840 Fr. De Smet met with Blue Feather and invited him on another missionary voyage.

"Blue Feather, you'll recall how a delegation from the western tribes called the Salish (or Flatheads) and their neighbors, the Nez Perce, came to Saint Louis and petitioned the Society of Jesus that a Black Robe return with them to teach their people about Jesus. They attempted first in 1831 to travel to St. Louis with their petition only to be massacred by hostile tribes and then again in 1839 reaching St. Louis unscathed. They had first heard about Jesus from a group of Iroquois fur trappers in 1824. The Iroquois people had been brought into the faith almost two hundred years earlier. So, the Society has decided to send a missionary and I was chosen to go to these tribes! Pete Gaucher will be going ahead of me with one of the Salish emissaries, who will prepare the way for us. And you, Blue Feather, if you can accept my invitation, will travel with me and the other emissaries, one from the Salish tribe and another from the Nez Perce tribe. Your mission will be to learn their languages during this long overland voyage, so that you can help me teach these people about God and his son. If you accept, you will be gone at least six months. So, pray on this and let me know your decision by Monday."

Blue Feather was taken aback by the offer of another missionary trip, this time a long one involving traveling overland by horse or wagon. Winnie will not be happy, that's for sure, he thought. He decided that he would discuss this with Mr. Mullanphy. He was wise and would know what to do.

On the following Saturday he was invited to supper at Mr. Mullanphy's mansion. After they ate, they went into the study as was Mr. Mullanphy's custom. They were not there more than five minutes when Blue Feather said, "Mr. Mullanphy, I have a dilemma. May I confide in you and get your advice?"

"Why certainly my boy! But what can old man like me advise you on?"

"You are wise, sir. And I trust you. My dilemma is this: Fr. De Smet would like me to go with him on a mission to the Salish and Nez Perce Indians. They sent a delegation to Saint Louis to see if the Society of Jesus would send them a black robe, i.e., a priest to teach them about Jesus. Fr. De Smet wants me to come with him to learn their language and then serve as a translator."

"Well, that is certainly important work, and you would be serving God by using your gift of languages."

"Yes, but it would mean being apart from Winnie for at least six months, and we promised each other that we would try to avoid separation."

"Son, it seems to me that when the good Lord has called you for a purpose, you should answer that call. Winnie will understand that. Say, I may have an idea! If Winnie is still serious about wanting to study nursing and midwifery, she can use this time to get her diploma from that school in Philadelphia!"

"But that would cost a lot of money that Winnie doesn't have. Besides, she has never traveled alone and would be nervous even thinking about it."

"My dear boy, I happen to know a certain fellow of the Mullanphy clan who would pay her tuition and her room and board. And he would even accompany her to the 'city of brotherly love' and make sure she has a good place to live while she is there. My sister Rose lives in Philadelphia and her home is less than a mile from that school. I know because she said so in a letter when the school was just opening. And she might even want to have Winnie as her guest."

"That is very generous of you, sir! But there is the question of whether this school would admit an Indian girl."

Mr. Mullanphy just smiled and said, "Don't ever forget that money talks and can be quite persuasive. We can get her admitted to that school, I have no doubt about it. Now, if I can arrange things just so, Winnie could get her letter of acceptance before you leave for the far west. Then she would not have reason to resent you for leaving her alone because she will have a chance to pursue her own dream."

♋   ♋   ♋

Mr. Mullanphy's prognostications had proven to be true -- Winnie was accepted to the nurse/midwifery school in Philadelphia. The magnanimous Irishman never told anyone about his generous donation to the school, which certainly had some role in her acceptance. The excellent recommendation from Dr. Caldwell also played a role. Then true to his word, Mr. Mullanphy accompanied Winnie to Philadelphia, and once his younger sister Rose met her, she wanted to have Winnie as a guest in her home.

Meanwhile, Blue Feather and Father De Smet were busy procuring all the supplies they would need for their mission. They were planning to join a wagon train of the American Fur Company which would start its journey in Westport, Missouri. They were told by the leader of the wagon train in a letter that they would need to have their own covered wagon and their own team of mules, horses, or oxen to pull it.

"We are going to need some expert advice, and the Society of Jesus will need to purchase a covered wagon. Tomorrow let's pay a visit to Mr. Wilhelm Edelmann at his livery stable and wagon dealership.

Mr. Edelmann was still new to the United States having emigrated in 1838 and he still had some difficulty finding his words in English. When Fr. De Smet and Blue Feather stepped into Mr. Edelmann's livery stable, he got up from his desk and extended his hand to Fr. De Smet.

"Guten Morgen, Pater De Smet. Es ist schön dich wieder zu sehen. Sind Sie hier, um eine Kutsche oder ein Pferd zu mieten?"

[Good morning, Father De Smet. It is good to see you again. Are you here to rent a carriage or horse?]

"Nein, Herr Edelman, ich bin daran interessiert, einen stabilen Wagen zu kaufen, der uns in die Rocky Mountains bringt. Wir brauchen auch ein Team von Pferden oder Maultieren."

[No, Mr. Edelman, I am interested in purchasing a sturdy wagon that will take us to the Rocky Mountains. We will also need a team of horses or mules. I am assuming you don't sell oxen.]

"Let me try to speak English. Vell, ve have drei, er, three wagens that you should consider. Let us walk out to my lot in back."

"This one is a Pennsylvania Conestoga wagon. It is a very sturdy wagon. The disadvantage is that it is heavier built than necessary, and you might need a team of six mules or oxen to pull it. Lighter in weight is this Studebaker, made in Indiana. A very fine wagon. And then here is a Murphy wagon, made here in Saint Louis. The Murphy wagon is the least expensive."

"Will the Murphy wagon be strong enough for the great distance over the rough terrain that we must travel?"

"Ja, the Murphy wagon will be sturdy enough to travel great distances over rough terrain. But you must take with you some essential spare parts. Of course, that is true of any wagon."

"Herr Edelmann, you must have outfitted many travelers to the frontier. Would you recommend horses, mules, or oxen for a team?"

"My preference is for mules, because they have better stamina than horses, require less grain, and are more sure-footed than horses when climbing. They got the reputation of being stubborn because will stop and look over a potentially dangerous situation before moving on. If the mule gets in it his mind that danger lies ahead, he will simply stop. However, mules will cost you $400 for a team of four."

"A lot of emigrants to the west have been choosing oxen. They are much cheaper, costing you about $100 for a team of four. Their disadvantage is that they are slower, going about 15 miles to the mule's 20 miles in a day. However, oxen are more reliable, less likely to run away and less likely to be stolen by marauding Indians. Also, oxen are better able to keep on pulling even when fatigued; and they are more likely to get by on whatever wild vegetation you happen across."

"But here is another consideration -- oxen need to be harnessed differently than horses or mules and it requires more time in the morning when you need to get going. If you get yourselves some oxen, I'll train you on how to harness them and other particulars of taking care of an oxen team."

"I'm assuming that you will not be traveling alone, right? Because that could be dangerous."

"We will be traveling in a caravan of 40 wagons."

"Then I recommend you talk to some savvy people here who have more first-hand knowledge about these things and find out if you can how many of your fellow travelers will be using mules versus oxen. It's better for you all to be equipped the same so that no one lags behind."

Father De Smet and Blue Feather decided they needed to think about their options and told Mr. Edelmann they would be back later with their decision about the wagon and the team.

Father De Smet and his protege walked to the Saint Louis College campus and discussed their options. Upon arriving at the college, a young priest ran up to Father De Smet with a message,

"Bon jour, Pere De Smet. There is a letter for you at the office," from Peter Gaucher in Westport. I thought I should make sure you picked it up as you prepare for your missionary journey west.

"Merci! That is kind of you to let me know" replied Father De Smet. After having lunch at the rectory, they walked back to Herr Edelmann's place of business. Father De Smet opened his letter as they walked.

"Oh, this is timely! Peter writes that the company usually uses mules on their journeys, especially if they are to climb some portion of the Rockies. So, it looks like we should buy mules."

At Herr Edelmann's they purchased a Murphy wagon, four mules, and some spare parts including tongues, axles and spokes. These were stored in an accessible wagonbox because sometimes repairs had to be completed quickly. Also stored were additional grease, ropes, and water. Father De Smet and Blue Feather were surprised when Herr Edelmann threw in the spare parts at no extra cost. "You are doing Gott's werk. This is my way of helping."

"Father, don't we need to stock up on food provisions for the trip, and cookware, plates, utensils, lanterns and oil, and blankets and other things for our long overland journey?"

"There are several items, you are correct. But my brothers at the Society of Jesus are going to provide what we need. However, we do need to arm ourselves in case we happen to be attacked by Indians who are not yet ready to hear the gospel! So let us go find a gunsmith who can sell us a pistol or musket."

Blue Feather was taken aback by the good Father's comments, but he shook it off. Of course, they would need to be able to defend themselves. They might find themselves trekking through some hostile areas.

Snapping out of his reverie, Blue Feather said, "Father, let's go to my uncle Pierre's house. He will know where we might get a good deal on a firearm."

"Oh, yes! Of course, does he live far from here?"

"No, not at all. We can walk there in 15 minutes."

When Pierre Chouteau recognized his nephew walking toward him, he dropped what he was doing, and ran to greet him. "Blue Feather, mon cher neveu. C'est si bon de vous revoir! Oh, excuse me! I just returned from Quebec where I had to speak nothing but French. If I started a conversation in English, the Quebecois would play dumb until I started over in French."

"It's good to see you too, Uncle Pierre! Let me introduce you to my professor, Father Pierre Jean De Smet. I'll be taking off some time from college to go with Father De Smet to the far west where we hope to establish a mission for the Indian tribes. We are leaving in a few days to join a wagon train of forty or so other wagons of the American Fur company."

"I am pleased to meet you, Father De Smet! Have you fellows traveled west before; I mean beyond the Omaha area?"

"No, it is the first time for both of us, and we have a lot to learn."

"Well, let me tell you that in addition to the physical challenge of the trek, you might run into some hostile Indians, that is, if your caravan is taking the southern route. I'm thinking particularly of the northern Comanche who are in a constant state of war with the Osage in the Kansas Territory. They are the worst of the tribes and are known for their brutality. They also have conflicts with the Arapaho and Cheyenne in Colorado. The name Comanche means something like 'enemies of everyone'. I expect that the men on this wagon train will be armed, and the two of you should be armed as well."

"I read just today that we will follow the Oregon trail which heads directly west into Kansas Territory and then veers north after about four days. There will be buffalo hunters on this wagon train who will be providing meat for the trek. Large herds of buffalo are expected to be found in Kansas Territory."

"Then you should be well-armed -- and I'm including you, Father, in this advice. The Comanche have no respect for white man's holy men. In fact, they might take special delight in capturing you and torturing you to death. On the positive side, you might earn your martyrdom."

"I assure you that I don't plan to make it easy for them, and I certainly don't want to hasten my departure from this earth; so tell us, if you will, where we might find suitable weapons."

Uncle Pierre was silent for a few seconds and looked down at his shoes deep in thought.

"Excuse me for a moment, please" and he disappeared into his house. Returning he had two firearms in his hands.

"Gentlemen, I'm going to lend you these two new firearms manufactured by Colt. Holding up the handgun, he said, "This here is a Colt Paterson five-shooter, a revolving pistol. This will be very handy in a battle in close quarters. The Comanche will swoop down at your wagon shooting arrows or guns, if they have managed to steal some from white settlers. Some will attempt to engage you in hand-to-hand combat so that they can count coup, that is, touch you before they kill you. Each coup is recorded as a notch on their coup stick. Coup is a game for the Comanche; in fact, you might say murder and rape are just sport for the Comanche. Their economic goal is to steal your horses, which they value above all other things."

"I also have this repeating rifle just released by Colt. It operates on the same principle as the revolving pistol. It holds six bullets. It is a more tempermental weapon and not all of the kinks have been worked out of it at this point, but the U.S. Army has been using it in the Seminole war. Have you ever fired a gun, Father?"

Father De Smet smiled and laughed and said, "Well, believe it or not, I actually joined the army in 1815 to defend my nation from Napoleon and his army at Wellington. I had learned how to fire a gun on the farm and then got some formal training and practice with the army. But then my parents realized where I had gone after I was missing for three weeks and they came and had me released from the service. I was only fourteen and half years old, and underage for military service!"

Laughing, Pierre Chouteau said, "It would seem that God was saving you for better works, for his purposes instead of man's!"

When Blue Feather and Fr. De Smet left Pierre Chouteau's home they were carrying a holstered Colt Paterson five-shooter and a leather scabbard holding the repeater rifle.

"Blue Feather, I want you to know that if we encounter Comanche or other hostile Indians, my first priority will be to share the gospel of Jesus Christ with them. I don't suppose you speak Comanche, or do you?"

"Not a word, Father! So, if you hope to engage a Comanche warrior in conversation, we should pray we encounter one who speaks English, or much more likely, Sioux. My Sioux is passable but far from fluent. But honestly, I don't think a Comanche warrior would give you the opportunity. He'll just want to kill you and take your scalp."

"Then we should pray for safety and for the opportunity to share the gospel."

CHAPTER SEVEN

wo days passed by quickly as Blue Feather and Fr. De
Smet acquired all the supplies they would need for their
missionary journey. They had picked up the Murphy
wagon and the four-mule team and drove it to each stop to purchase food items, cookware, metal plates and utensils, grain for
the mules, blankets, pup tents, tools for repairs and construction, and ammunition for their guns. Thus loaded, they began
their journey to Westport at first light the next morning. At the
college where they had been staying, the faculty and some of
the students woke up early to send them off with a prayer and
blessing.

Their first stop was the Osage village of Blue Feather's grand-
parents and mother. His mother didn't say much, but she hugged
her son and kissed him wishing him a safe journey. Grandfather
appeared with a new bow and a quiver full of arrows. "You might
need these in Kansas Territory. You will probably pass Council
Grove where the Osage of the area have agreed to give white settlers free passage. If they ask who you are, tell them who your
grandfather is. The older men might remember me. Anyway, if
you speak to them in their native Osage language, they will welcome you."

Turning to Father De Smet, grandfather said, "Father, you
have been a good teacher of my grandson. I want you to have this
riding mule. Her name is Lizette."

Father De Smet was surprised by the generous gift and said,
"Grandfather, thank you! I will take good care of her."

"One word of advice: Do not put a horse saddle on her. She will only move if you put this lightweight saddle blanket on her. That is the Indian way."

The Salish (Flathead) and Nez Perce emissaries had been staying with the Osage and joined Blue Feather and Fr. De Smet. Each of them was pulling a travois with their travel teepees and other supplies. Other than the teepees, they traveled light.

It was almost noon on March 27 when they began their trek to Westport to join the wagon train of the American Fur Company. The Missouri weather was still cold, not quite spring.

The trip to Westport was uneventful. Along the way, one or more of the travelers went off to hunt for dinner. The game was usually quite small, being rabbits, prairie chickens, and some waterfowl such as ducks or geese. But one day, the Nez Perce brave returned with a large deer, which would feed them for at least three days. This was fortuitous because the next day a late snowstorm hit central Missouri, and the trek slowed considerably. The first day of the storm they had no choice but to drive their wagon into a grove of trees and set up camp to wait out the storm. A cold driving snow made starting a fire more than challenging. Fortunately, the Nez Perce and Flathead braves who were leading them were more familiar with camping under these conditions and helped the two Missourians get things going. That night the Indians set up their teepees and gave one to Fr. De Smet to share with Blue Feather while they shared the other. Inside the teepees they were able to start fires and exhaust the smoke through the vents in the teepee. It actually was fairly comfortable especially since the Indians lent them buffalo skin blankets.

The next morning, after some pemmican and coffee, they ventured forth through the snow-covered trail. Although the snow fall had stopped, the trail was covered with at least six inches of snow and the mules trudged laboriously through it. The next day brought much warmer weather and the snow melted leaving a slushy and then muddy trail. Travel was not much faster than the day before.

After a few days of warming weather with sunshine the trail dried considerably, but then the April showers began, and travel slowed down again. The Indian braves did not complain about the weather, but Blue Feather could see that they were more bothered by the driving rain than they were by the snow. The rain not only meant a slow muddy trail but also more difficulties hunting game because the animals tried to find dry spots and hide out until the rain passed. Then Blue Feather recalled that fishing during rain can be quite rewarding. The rain tends to wash insects from the riverbanks into the water making something like a smorgasbord for trout and bass. At this point they were just a couple miles south from the Missouri River, so Blue Feather went fishing. He rode Lizette so that he could later catch up with the other travelers as they trudged onwards. A couple of hours later he caught up with the slowly moving wagon holding a bucket with two trout, a bass, and a catfish. His companions were all smiles.

The travelers reached Westport (which would later become Kansas City) on April 27. They found the caravan of the American Fur Company with ease and started to restock their wagon with food items and ammunition. Fr. De Smet and Blue Feather drove their wagon to their designated position in the long line of wagons, and then went looking for the caravan pilot, a man called Captain Jedidiah (Jed) Gregg. Captain Gregg was something of an adventurer/explorer as well as an amateur botanist and zoologist who like to catalog the flora and fauna he encountered on his journeys. His interest in the west was whetted by his reading of the report of the voyage of Meriwether Lewis and William Clark as a boy.

Captain Gregg was only 35 years of age, but he looked older than men of that age who confined themselves to the city. With his tanned and weather-lined face expressing some skepticism he appeared to size up the newcomers and said, "To be honest with you Padre, we've never had a priest or preacher man on this kind of trek before. You know there is a chance we'll encounter some hostile Indians along the way. Will you be ready and willing to defend yourself? Blue Feather was a bit agitated and started to blurt out a retort, but Fr. De Smet held him back. "You need not be concerned with us, Captain. Back in my native Belgium, I defended my nation against Napolean's army when I was only 15. I've known how to handle a musket since I was 10 years of age."

"Well, then keep in mind that the Indians who attack us will be on horseback and will charge us with lances and with arrows. An Indian can shoot five arrows in the time a white man can fire and reload his musket."

This time Blue Feather responded, "I will be using my bow during any skirmish, and if I must, a repeating pistol in close quarters. Fr. De Smet will use a repeating Colt rifle."

"Really? I've read about those repeater rifles. Still kind of experimental if you ask me; but it seems that the U.S. Army is having some success with them in the war with the Seminoles. All right then, gentlemen. We'll be leaving at first light on April 30, so make double sure you have all your provisions packed up."

When they had left Captain Gregg, Blue Feather asked Fr. De Smet, "Wasn't that a bit of a lie when you said you had fought against Napolean's army?"

Fr. De Smet showed a faint smile and said, "Blue Feather, that wasn't a lie, it was merely a clerical error."

It took Blue Feather a few seconds before he caught his mentor's meaning, but then he smiled and shook his head at the pun.

Some days later the caravan reached Council Grove. A party of twelve or so mounted Indian braves blocked their path on the trail. Blue Feather was riding Lizette at the time, and he surmised what was happening. "Fr. De Smet, I think those braves blocking the way are Osage warriors. I should ride up ahead and see if I can assist the captain."

Blue Feather rode up to the head of the column and shouted out the traditional greeting among the Osage. (In Osage) "Hello, brothers. I am Blue Feather, grandson of Standing Bear, of the Osage nation."

The Osage braves looked at each other, and then the spokesman said, "Greetings, Blue Feather, Standing Bear was a wise and mighty warrior. Is he well and still farming?"

"Yes, he is still strong and working hard. Can you tell us if there is trouble ahead on this trail?"

"Yes, we were trying to tell your captain that, but my English was failing me. The Osage are having trouble with the Comanche nation which is trying to drive the Osage and our relatives the Kansa out of their territories. Our hunting parties have been attacked by their raiding parties and wagon trains have been attacked with no reason except the Comanche like to kill and steal horses. Seeing as how the Comanche are making trouble, we want to ride with you on your travels through lands we consider our own."

Blue Feather translated for the wagon train captain, "The Osage spokesman is White Eagle. He says his warriors will accompany us through the lands they claim because the Comanche are on the warpath these days trying to drive out the Osage and Kansa."

"Tell him we are much obliged and that we will heading north by northwest now."

Blue Feather translated for White Eagle, who responded haltingly in English, "Much danger lies in your path. That is land that the Comanche will die fighting for."

The captain turned to Blue Feather, "Son, pass the word down the column, that all men should have their weapons loaded and at the ready. There could be Injun trouble."

Blue Feather did as he was requested, and when he came to Fr. De Smet's wagon he told his mentor the whole story.

"So, you don't think this is right time to teach the Comanche about God's love and the sacrifice of His son?"

"Father, they will swoop down in force, ambushing us when we pass by a grove of trees where they have been hiding. They will not be in the mood for talk."

Father De Smet gave a wistful smile, then looked up to the sky and appeared to offer a silent prayer. "Perhaps you're are right Blue Feather, but I am praying otherwise. We can't know beforehand how the Holy Spirit will move us or them."

A couple of days later the Salish (Flat Head) emissary named Kajika (Walks without Sound), and the Nez Perce emissary called Shariki (Coyote) announced that they were going to hunt for game. Fr. De Smet decided to go with them, riding Lizette, and declined to take his repeating rifle. Blue Feather just assumed that his mentor would arm himself and was surprised when he found Fr. De Smet's rifle still in the wagon. He was alarmed by the idea of the priest venturing out into potentially dangerous territory unarmed, but there wasn't much he could do because no one was sure of the direction thc hunters had taken. Blue Feather decided that he just had to wait and pray that everyone would be safe. In the meantime, the caravan had stopped to make some repairs on two wagons that broke an axle.

Things did not go well for the hunting party. Kajika and Shariki were hunting with bow and arrow to avoid drawing attention to themselves with the noise of gunfire just in case there were hostile Indians in the vicinity. They went hours without finding significant game but then happened on a large whitetail buck drinking from a stream. Kajika and Shariki both shot at the buck, and it fell after a short run with arrows in its gut. But as they drew up to their kill, they saw that the buck had three arrows protruding from its gut, the two they shot on one side, and one on the other side shot by another hunter. A young brave was kneeling beside their kill already field dressing the deer as Kajika and Shariki pulled up. The young brave was not of their party, but a local Indian, if that is not an oxymoron, because Plains Indians were often on the move.

The young brave became agitated at the sight of intruders, and he whistled and cried out in his Comanche language for backup. Kajika and Shariki understood enough of the Comanche language to realize they were about to be taken captive or killed and looked at each other in alarm. Both Indians spoke some Shoshone because the Shoshone were a neighboring tribe. The Comanche language was derived from the Shoshone.

Within seconds a band of twelve Comanche warriors on horseback swooped down on Kajika, Shariki, and Fr. De Smet, knocking them down from their steeds. They tied their hands together and forced them to follow the horses on foot, occasionally prodding them along with their lances.

Three hours later in the early afternoon, the three captives, bleeding and bruised, stumbled into the Comanche camp along with their captors. However, arriving at the camp did not mean that things would get any easier for them. To amuse themselves the Comanches made their captives run naked through a gauntlet. Braves formed a tunnel through which the captives were forced to run. Each brave was armed with some kind weapon to strike or poke the captives with; none were intended to wield a lethal blow, just considerable pain. The Comanches found the cries of their victims quite amusing, and they laughed uproariously when Shariki stumbled and fell. If a captive fell, he would be whipped all the harder until he got up and resumed the course. The weapons were sticks, shortened lances, war clubs, torches, and something like a cat-of-nine tails. When he saw the latter, Fr. De Smet mused to himself that the Comanches must have learned something from European culture. After all, Roman soldiers had tortured Jesus with such a weapon.

Shariki was not a young man. He was well into his fifties; and when he fell Fr. De Smet and Kajika had to pull him up. Their efforts earned them some extra blows.

The torturers decided to break for dinner, but not before they stripped and staked down the captives in spread-eagle fashion on the ground. Of course, the captives were not fed. Later the captors returned to put hot coals on the captives' private areas. The chief of this band was impressed with the captives' stoicism but was especially astonished by Fr. De Smet's behavior. He did not cry out in pain to plea for mercy like most weak white men. Instead, he repeatedly prayed and sang hymns to his god.

There was a white captive boy of about ten years of age who apparently had been adopted by the chief. He was not treated like the native Comanche boys. With his blond hair and blue eyes, he would never be fully accepted into the tribe, but he was useful to the chief. The chief called him to his side and told him to find out who the white captive was, and why he was so brave.

The boy walked over to where Fr. De Smet was stretched out and knelt down by his head. He spoke haltingly in English: "The chief wants to know why you don't cry out in pain like the others."

Fr. De Smet detected an accent, and he asked the boy "I will tell you the reason for my hope and peace, but first I want to know your name". And then he repeated himself in German.

The boy's eyes lit up with surprise and their conversation continued in German.

"My name is Johannes, and I am from Friesland. The Comanches attacked our wagon train in Texas four years ago. My father and mother were killed, but only after my mother was raped by four different men. They let me live and took me captive, wanting to turn me into a savage like them. But I still pray to the one true God for rescue because of the evil things they have done."

"My son, I am Father Pierre Jean De Smet, a Catholic priest. Tell the chief that I have hope and peace because I know and serve the one true God who created all things, and that he knows all things. He knows the number of hairs on my head and knows when a single sparrow falls from the sky. Nothing escapes his attention."

"I will tell him that! But, Father, if I can help you escape tonight will you take me with you?"

"Yes, Johannes. I promise."

The boy ran back to the chief who said, "You talked with him a long time. What did you find out?"

"Chief Takotay, the white man is a great shaman of the white man's god. He has powerful medicine. His god knows all and sees all. Not even a single sparrow can fall from the sky without his God knowing it. In the past this great god, whom the whites claim is the only god, had caused a great flood to destroy all life except for one man and his family and the animal pairs they brought onto a great canoe with them. This same god caused fire to come down and destroy two wicked cities. And most recently, this god sent his own son to earth to live among us and teach us the way to live. When shamans of a false god had the son killed, he rose from the dead after three days. The white man's name is Father De Smet and the Comanche cannot kill his spirit which is eternal and should his physical body die, he will live on with the father, son, and holy spirit in heaven. That is why he has hope and peace."

"Why did this man leave the comforts and safety of the white man's city? I have seen the great city called Saint Looey and its great stone places of worship that soar into the air a hundred feet."

"Chief, he says his god wants him to teach all Indian nations about god the father, god the son, and god the holy spirit. The white man's god draws all mankind to himself and will not rest until all knees shall bow before him."

"I have never heard before of any god with so much power, or of any man who would risk his life to serve his god. Go now and cut his bindings. Here, give him back his black robe and his talismans (speaking of his rosary, Bible, and crucifix), and bring him to my teepee. We will give him food and drink. I must hear more about his god."

The boy did as he was told and took the liberty of bringing a bowl of water and a cloth to clean the holy man's face and wounds. Fr. De Smet smiled as the boy told him what he had told the chief.

"Johannes, you have served our God well today!"

Father De Smet was interrupted by a plea from Shariki, "Father, please administer the last rites to me, I will die soon!"

Father De Smet quickly donned his black robe and knelt by Shariki and heard his confession, led him in prayer, and administered the last rites in Latin. When he finished, Shariki looked at Father De Smet and said, "Thank you, Father. Now Lord, into your hands I commit my spirit." Then he closed his eyes and died.

"Shariki has now passed from this world into the next, from a world of torment, disease, and death to an everlasting paradise with Jesus."

All of the Comanches who looked on at these final moments of Shariki's life, viewed Fr. De Smet with fear and trembling; and as Johannes led him to the chief's teepee, they gave him wide berth.

♋ ♋ ♋

Meanwhile, back at the wagon train which had not moved for hours, Blue Feather and others who knew Fr. De Smet and his two Indian companions grew very anxious. Blue Feather was with Captain Gregg who was standing on a wagon seat surveying the area with spyglasses. "I think I see columns of smoke, as if from several cook fires. Perhaps those columns of smoke are coming from an Indian village, not a permanent village but more likely a temporary encampment. If our friends have been captured by hostile Indians, and I'll bet they are Comanches, this is where they would be held."

"Captain, I volunteer to lead a posse of men, armed to the teeth, to that encampment. We can rescue them before the Comanche kill them, but we must act quickly."

Captain Gregg stared at Blue Feather for a couple of seconds and then without another word, blew a whistle which was his signal for the men of fighting age to assemble.

When the men were assembled Captain Gregg said, "Men, we have reason to believe that Father De Smet and his two Indian companions have been captured by hostile Indians. In the distance you can see columns of smoke rising from cook fires. We are guessing that is where they are being held. I need fifteen men to ride with me and Blue Feather to this Indian camp to rescue our friends. Come armed and ready to fight! And I'll need another fifteen men to be armed and ready to defend this wagon train. So, if you volunteer for the rescue mission raise your hand."

A couple of men raised their hands right away, and then gradually the number of raised hands increased to thirteen.

"OK, we've got fifteen men now, including Blue Feather and myself. Hurry now and get your weapons and horses and we'll meet at the head of the train. Once we leave, I want the wagons drawn into a circle and ready for an Indian attack."

As the rescue posse rode out, Blue Feather looked at the collection of men who had volunteered. He saw that the majority of the men were young, probably still in their twenties. But there were a few who were thirty or over, and two who were probably in their forties. Whether or not they were experienced Indian fighters he did not know. But he did know that they were brave men to risk their lives in this manner.

Back at the Comanche encampment, people were getting nervous when they saw the sky turning a sickening green and dark wall clouds forming. The first trouble they had was a hailstorm. Large hailstones fell, driving the Indians into their teepees. The chief called Johannes to his side and asked him "Can the white priest ask his God to save us from this storm from Manakyia?"

"I will go ask him now!"

When Fr. De Smet heard the chief's question he told Johannes, "Tell the chief that my God is angry with the Comanche and that if the chief would let his captives go free, God might spare your people. But the chief must do this immediately."

When the boy told the chief this message the chief said, "Hurry back to the white priest of the angry god and tell him that he and his Indian companion must take their steeds and flee back to their white man's camp, lest we all die here."

Finding Fr. De Smet, the boy said, "The chief said we must leave immediately. I'll go get three horses, well two horses and your mule. I remember which horses your Indian friends were riding. I will ride Shariki's horse and go with you!"

Only minutes later, Fr. De Smet, Kajika, and Johannes were riding furiously back to the wagon train. About midway they encountered Blue Feather's posse and they were all relieved.

"Captain, it is good that we were freed from captivity, but we lost Shariki who died of his wounds suffered during brutal torture. But God showed his mercy to this boy Johannes who had been a captive for four years. I can tell you more later, but we must get back to the wagon train before the storm reaches its full fury," said Fr. De Smet.

They galloped to the wagon train and sped through the narrow gap that had been left for their return. Dismounting quickly, the captain sought the wagon train physician, who fortunately was still sober. Dr. Stokes examined Fr. De Smet and Kajika and treated their wounds. "I want you fellows to take it easy for a few days. Ride in a wagon and give your bodies a rest. The only pain relief I can provide is this laudanum and Bourbon whiskey. We'll use the laudanum only if the bourbon doesn't work. Laudanum is habit forming."

Captain Gregg took an interest in Johannes and told him, "Come with me, Johannes, there are some people I want you to meet who will be very interested in you."

The boy simply nodded, yes. He figured that whoever takes him in would have to be better than the Comanche chief, who treated him as a slave.

They walked over to a large wagon that served as a chuck wagon for the captain, the doctor, and company employees. The two cooks were Gertrude and Heinrich De Jong. Gertrude was a tall, big-boned woman with blonde hair pulled back into a ponytail. She was what people would say a handsome woman, not pretty in the usual feminine way, but attractive. Heinrich was a slender man with red hair and spectacles. Besides being a quartermaster and cook for the wagon train, he played the fiddle to entertain the travelers. They worked as a couple hiring themselves out to wagon trains carrying goods and immigrants to various points west. Two years prior to this trip they had lost their nine-year-old son, Otto, to the measles.

Gertrude looked at Johannes and said in Frisian, "Oh good Gott in heaven! Would you look at this hungry young man? The captain said he's an orphan who was a captive of those Indians for four years. He needs a meal and then a bath and some fresh clothes." Then switching to English, she said, "Oh, where are my manners? I said the captain told us you were an orphan who was living with those Indians."

Johannes smiled broadly and said, "I understood everything you said! I was born in Friesland. My family name is De Vries."

From that day on Johannes lived with the De Jong family and became their son. Johannes helped fill the void they felt with the loss of their son, and they came to love him dearly.

Captain Gregg rode through the camp telling everyone to eat a quick cold meal before the storm hit. The wind was picking up now with gusts upwards of fifty miles per hour. By the time the captain returned to his wagon, the thunderstorm with rain was already starting and quickly turning into a heavy downpour.

Fr. De Smet, Kajika, and Blue Feather sat inside their covered wagon on top of cases of canned goods, books, and equipment.

They cinched up the canvas openings as best they could, but wind and rain still blew in making for a wet and chilly experience.

"If this tornado touches down here at our camp, we might have a few wagons get blown over; but I fear more for the Comanche camp with people living in those teepees," said Fr. De Smet.

"Father, those teepees are sturdier than you might think," said Kajika. "And you might not have realized this, but the footprint of a teepee is actually an oval, not a circle, and Indians generally orient their teepees so that the wind travels around the long edges of the teepee. These plains Indians have weathered storms like this for countless generations, so they know what to do. But, heck, anything can happen in a tornado."

"You were wise to speak in terms of God to the chief. The Comanche and the Kiowa believe that the tornado is the work of a god called Manakyia. As the legend goes on the earth before there were any people, the animals considered the horse to be a god. There were four horses, and the other animals were able to capture one of them as it drank from a lake. But one was not enough. They wanted another horse, so they made a figure of a horse out clay and stuck hair on it from the buffalo. When they saw how ugly it was, they decided they must destroy it lest it run loose and attack them. So, they attempted to drown it in the lake. But once it hit the water, its hind quarters twisted into a type of cone-shaped tail, and it flew out of the water high into the sky. Ever since then whenever man has done something that displeases this god, it comes back and tries to sweep everything away with its awful tail. Today we see the god's tail as the funnel cloud."

The next morning everyone got up and surveyed the damage left by the storm. One wagon had been blown over and its neighbor had lost its canvas cover and had its contents strewn about. But no life was lost. The mules and horses had huddled closely together with their butts to the wind as in the manner of wild horses on the plains. Some instincts don't die with domestication.

Fr. De Smet went to Captain Gregg and announced that he wanted to say a mass of Thanksgiving to God for their good fortune during the storm. Captain Gregg said, "I don't know how many of these men are Catholic, but I have no objection. Heinrich De Jong had been nearby and overheard their conversation. "Forgive me for intruding, but Fr. De Smet, Gertrude and I are Catholics, and we would welcome the opportunity to hear mass. Gertrude has some bread you can use for communion. I'll go spread the word now. Are you thinking of starting mass in half an hour?

"Yes, that will work out for me and please encourage all Christians to come, not just Catholics."

The De Jongs set up their table to be used as an altar and Fr. De Smet then said his first Mass on this long trek they were facing. The sermon was brief and focused on thanksgiving to God for seeing them through the tornado without major mishap or injury. The service ended with a prayer for continued protection from storms and hostile Indians.

Shortly afterwards, the travelers broke camp and resumed their trek. The wagon train continued its slow (at most three miles per hour) journey stopping only for supper.

CHAPTER EIGHT

Fr. De Smet and Kajika rode in the covered wagon, this being somewhat more comfortable than riding horseback given their injuries at the hands of the Comanches. The two men were healing slowly, especially the delicate parts where the hot coals were dropped on their bare skin. Blue Feather rode Lizette who initially was somewhat skittish because of the ordeal of the storm but she settled down as the routine of the trip was resumed.

Their northwesterly route would take the wagon train through Sioux hunting grounds in Nebraska Territory. What they didn't know was that they were on a collision course with a gigantic buffalo herd and that the Sioux were not in the mood to share.

Some of the men traveling with the wagon train were experienced buffalo hunters and when the large herd was first seen, two of them, Ned Jenkins and Isaiah Griswell, enthusiastically embarked on a hunt, taking a wagon with them to carry back the carcass. Captain Gregg approved of their mission because the travelers needed meat and this herd was an obvious windfall.

Although Blue Feather had hunted buffalo with the Osage, he did not join the hunt, knowing how grisly the business of killing a buffalo, skinning it, and butchering it, could be.

The Sioux were hunting the buffalo from the eastern edge of the herd and the travelers from the southern edge. Despite their approaches to the herd being from mostly distinct directions, there eventually was a point at which the two groups encountered each other. Neither party was happy to meet the other. A dispute emerged over a killed bull which had both an arrow and two bullet holes in it. The Sioux brave was convinced that the arrow was the fatal blow; but the white hunters held that their two bullet holes were closer to the bull's lung. The simple and reasonable solution of dividing the kill was not an option.

The argument escalated into a knife fight. Ned Jenkins had a long-bladed Bowie knife, and the Sioux Brave had his hunting knife. Ned Jenkins, at six-foot, two inches, had the height and reach advantage over his five-foot six-inch opponent. Neither opponent appeared to be winning until the brave took a wild jab with his knife. His jab missed, but as Ned sidestepped the blade, he swung his blade at the brave's throat. His blade sliced open the carotid artery and the brave immediately knew was dying. He collapsed and began to bleed out.

Ned looked over at Isaiah who was staring with wide eyes at the dying Indian. Isaiah said, "Ned, forget the buffalo meat! We've got to hightail it back to the wagons. This Injun wasn't alone out here on the prairie -- any minute now his friends are going to show up and we'll be invited to a scalping party!"

The two hunters jumped on their wagon and drove their team hard back to the wagon train. They yelled "Captain Gregg, Captain Gregg! Circle the wagons, Circle the wagons! We're going to be attacked by Injuns any minute now!"

Captain Gregg quickly mobilized his wagon drivers and within minutes a tight circle of covered wagons was accomplished. None too soon because when he looked north, he could see a large war party heading their way just over the horizon. He probably didn't need to say this, but he did anyway: "Load up and ready your weapons!"

The war party, numbering around twenty braves, arrived and immediately began circling the ring of wagons. They were armed with bows and arrows and tomahawks and knives for close hand-to-hand combat, which was preferred because of the opportunity to count coup. Touching one's opponent before killing him (coup) was considered an honor all braves could aspire to. It made warfare something of a game for them.

Father De Smet was with Blue Feather when the attack started. He was having second thoughts about shooting at other human beings. He handed Blue Feather the repeating rifle and said, "Here my son, you should use this weapon. My heart is not in it. It's one thing to shoot at a varmint getting into a man's stored grain, as I did back in Belgium; it's another thing entirely when the target is another man. I will stay by your side and reload for you as needed."

Blue Feather accepted the weapon with a nod and began firing at the warriors as they rode by. He tried to time it so that he would shoot as soon as possible after he saw them launch an arrow. His aim with the rifle was astonishingly good.

In some ways the attacking Indians had an advantage in that they could shoot three or four arrows in the time it took for a white defender to fire and reload his weapon. In addition, the Indian presented a harder to hit moving target. Both sides suffered some casualties, and some were fatal. Some braves became bold and dismounted and tried to crawl under a wagon to attack their opponent with a tomahawk or knife. One unfortunate brave chose to crawl under Gertrude's chuck wagon and was rewarded with a heavy blow from an iron skillet. One could hear the skillet ring out and some travelers of the American Fur Company claimed they hear the crunch of a skull cracking.

As was usually the case, the Indians quit their attack when they saw that a clear victory was not attainable. Live to fight another day. They had lost five of their twenty-one braves, and the white travelers lost two men to well-placed arrows.

Gertrude De Jong decided to treat the young brave she had walloped for his concussion before releasing him to his people. Fr. De Smet tried to befriend the young brave, who did not appear to be more than seventeen years old. For his part, Captain Gregg decided that they would stay encamped overnight and then see if the Indians would attack again in the morning. They would be ready to put up a good fight if it proved necessary.

Blue Feather and Kajika stopped by the captive to see if they could learn anything about the identity of his tribe and what motivated the attack. The young brave looked up with some surprise when he saw that his visitors were Indians like him, or at least one them was. He hadn't decided whether Blue Feather was an Indian or simply a dark-complected white. He had heard that not all whites were pale, like Gertrude and Heinrich and their son, Johannes, who were keeping him captive but feeding him well. Kajika asked him what his tribe was by pointing to himself and saying "Salish" and then pointing to Blue Feather and saying "Osage". The young brave appeared to know these tribe names. Then Kajika pointed to him and said, "Pawnee?" "Omaha?" and other tribal names. But the young man shook his head to these. Then when Kajika said Dakota Sioux, the young man pointed to his own chest and said, "Dakota Sioux." Through some use of plains Indian sign language, the closest thing to a lingua franca there was among the many tribes of Indians, there were additional exchanges which led them to learn that his name was Gray Bull and that his original tribe was the Cheyenne. He had been captured during a raid as a young boy. When he heard that they were headed to Wyoming Territory, he got excited, and asked to come with them.

The trek was uneventful for some weeks. Hunters were able to provide the wagon train with buffalo meat, and no one went hungry. But eventually they encountered a new tribe, the Arapaho, who was not happy to see the wagon train, which they perceived to be a threat to their possession of the land and as competition for the buffalo.

As the wagon train approached the North Platte River their progress was observed by some Arapaho Indians crouching on a high bluff overlooking the river. Upon reaching the river the wagon train stopped and preparations were made for an encampment there overnight.

Many buffalo stopped by the North Platte River for water and that made certain points along the river excellent hunting grounds. Obviously, the long-time residents or visitors to this location knew of this and would wait in hiding for the shaggy beasts in the groves of trees lining the river. This is when the Arapaho hunters first encountered hunters from the wagon train face-to-face. There was a shaky and tense start to their first meeting. Fortunately, one of the wagon train's hunters was Gray Bull who was fluent in the sign language of the Indians in the Great Plains, and he recalled some Cheyenne words that the Arapaho Indians understood. The gist of their conversation was that the Arapaho were concerned that the powerful rifles used by the white hunters would cause the herd to stampede. The Arapaho used bows and arrows and could silently kill dozens of buffaloes without alarming the herd.

The presence of Gray Bull and other Indians from the wagon train, namely, Blue Feather and Kajika, somewhat mollified the Arapaho's suspicion of the newcomers.

Their discussion in mostly sign language concluded with the hunters from the wagon train offering to use only bows and arrows when they hunted and leaving the buffalo hides for the Arapaho, who had more need of them than the travelers.

With this somewhat uneasy peace established, Father De Smet decided that the Arapaho nation might be ready to respond to the gospel. He told Blue Feather and Kajika of his desire to make first contact. Kajika and Blue Feather listened to the priest's passionate argument for sharing the gospel and tried to urge caution and dissuade the priest. But Fr. De Smet said that he was putting his full reliance on God -- that "if God is for you, who can stand against you?" Unsuccessful in changing his mind, Kajika and Blue Feather decide to go with him.

They had only a general sense of the location of the Arapaho village. This was not a permanent village, but instead an encampment of buffalo hunters and their families. The women took charge of skinning and processing the buffalo hides, and so were included in the hunt.

The threesome noticed a column of smoke rising in the distance and directed their steeds on course to what they thought was a village. As they approached the village, they realized that they had stumbled upon the Arapaho being attacked by a hostile tribe. They heard no gunfire, only the screams of women and children as they were captured.

So far, they had gone unnoticed and made for the woods to hide until the attack was over and then render aid if they could. But then they saw a group of six riders headed their way. They urged Father De Smet to go deeper into the woods and to stay quiet. Blue Feather and Kajika decided to lead the party away from Fr. De Smet, who would not take up arms to defend himself.

Their plan was not a total success. Four of the riders took off in chase of Blue Feather and Kajika. Kajika shouted to Blue Feather, "Head for that high ground with the boulders. Dismount as soon as you reach the boulders and take up a firing position using the boulders as cover!"

They had a good start on the Indian raiders and were able to take cover and start to lay down fire while their pursuers were still climbing the hill. Two of the raiders were killed right away with bullets from Blue Feather's repeating rifle. Kajika critically wounded a third with a well-placed arrow, and the fourth broke away from the fight to retrieve his fallen comrade. He then turned tail and fled from the attack.

Blue Feather turned to Kajika, "We need to find Fr. De Smet! The other two raiders might have found him, and God only knows what they would do to him!" As they approached Fr. De Smet's location, Blue Feather heard voices speaking excitedly in the Sioux language, giving orders to Fr. De Smet, who didn't know the language. Translated they said, "Give us your mule and you won't die, white man. We can easily kill you because you have no weapon!"

Blue Feather and Kajika heard this as they approached a clearing in the woods. Still some twenty yards away, they could see that a huge gray dog (or was it a wolf?) was standing between Fr. De Smet and the angry raiders threatening him. When one of the Indians raised his bow to shoot Fr. De Smet, the animal became enraged and leaped up to grab the Indian by the arm with his teeth. The Indian screamed as the animal savagely tore into him. Fr. De Smet whistled and said, "Enough! Let him go!" Amazingly the animal released the man and went back to Fr. De Smet and stood next to him. The Indian, still with terror in his eyes, scrambled up, and shouted in Sioux, "Shaman or devil, I don't know, but your medicine is very powerful!" And then he ran away in search of his horse.

The animal, which appeared to be a wolf-dog hybrid, was more than four feet tall at the shoulder, but as gentle as a kitten when the priest was no longer threatened. The wolf-dog looked up at Fr. De Smet and leaned into him as if he wanted to be petted. So, Fr. De Smet obliged his request.

At this point, Blue Feather and Kajika entered the clearing and the wolf-dog sat up and wagged his tail in a friendly manner. Blue Feather said, "Father De Smet, we saw what happened! Your new friend appeared just at the right moment!"

"Yes, and I suspect this is no ordinary animal. He is *Un ange sous la forme d'un* énorme *chien-loup* (an angel in the form of an enormous wolf-dog). I am sure that the good Lord sent him to me. If he chooses to follow us, I will call him Grigio, the Gray one."

"It sure looks like he likes you! He can probably find his own food if he chooses to follow the wagon train."

"Yes, then I will not shoo him away. Besides, perhaps God has more in store for us that Grigio can help us with!"

With the Arapaho village being destroyed with only a few survivors, Fr. De Smet, Blue Feather, and Kajika, found themselves doing more first aid and burial details than anything else. Kajika described the situation to Fr. De Smet,

"Father, I have studied the relations among the tribes in these parts. The Arapaho are not yet open to the gospel. They have always been a warlike people who have various "military societies" according to the age and accomplishment of their braves. The Arapaho have fought against other tribes both near and far. They have fought with the Pawnee, Omaha, Osage, Ponca, and Kaw to the east. To the north of their territory, they fought with the Crow, Blackfoot, Gros Ventre, Flathead, Arikara, Assinboine, Cree of both the woods and the plains, the Saulteaux (plains Ojibwa), and the Stoney tribes. To the west they fought with the Shoshone, Ute, and to the south they fought with the Navajo, Apache, Jiracilla Apache, and various Pueblo tribes. The only tribe that I know of which they haven't made their enemy is the Cheyenne. The Cheyenne impressed me as being open to the gospel, at least curious. If the Cheyenne can be brought to Christ, then perhaps the Arapaho will become more open to the gospel."

Fr. De Smet was lost in thought for a few seconds, then sighed and said, "Then we must make the most of every minute with the Cheyenne, perhaps preparing them for the mission that we as outsiders cannot carry out."

When the Arapaho buffalo hunters returned to their village they were dismayed by the loss of life and property to the raiders. The old men who had stayed behind reported that it was some variety of Sioux who had attacked them, and afterwards, two Indians of different tribes appeared along with a white man in a black robe and cared for their wounds. The Arapaho appreciated their help, and though they didn't say this explicitly, they were softening toward whatever the white man's God might offer them. Fr. De Smet, through the sign language of Kajika, told them that he must return to his wagon train, but that he would return to them someday.

⊗ ⊗ ⊗

The American Fur Company wagon train continued its trek to the planned rendezvous point on Green River in Wyoming. Blue Feather spent his time learning how to scout and navigate from Kajika and learning his Salish language. From Gray Bull, Blue Feather learned the Cheyenne language and some Dakota Sioux.

Finally, after two months of travel, on June 30th, the wagon train arrived at their destination. To his great surprise, Fr. De Smet found ten warriors from the Salish and Nez Perces nations waiting for him to escort him to the main Salish camp.

"Greetings, Father! We were sent here to help you find your way to the Salish! We asked our Father in heaven for a black robe and our prayers have been answered after years of waiting!"

"I am truly glad to be here for this opportunity to share the gospel with you and to help you grow in faith! To help me in my ministry I asked my young friend Blue Feather on this great journey. He belongs to the Osage nation, but he has been learning the languages of many Indian nations, including the Salish, so that he can help me explain God's word to you."

"Father, you should rest here a few days before we begin our trek to the Salish. We have heard how the Comanches had captured you and tortured you. This is shameful behavior that neither we the Salish or our brothers, the Nez Perces, would ever have engaged in. Now, before we proceed, please give your body some time to recover."

"I will both rest and prepare for the next stage of my journey. This Sunday I want to offer a mass to our Lord in thanksgiving for keeping us safe in our journey thus far. However, I am sad to report that we lost Shariki of the Nez Perce to the Comanches. He died from injuries sustained during torture. He lived long enough to ask for and receive the Last Rites and now he rests with our Lord in heaven. He died for his faith, and so he may be honored as a martyr."

Fr. De Smet, Blue Feather, and Kajika spent a few days at the Green River Rendezvous, and then they left with their escort headed for the main camp of Salish and Pend d' Oreills (who spoke a dialect of the Salish language) at Pierre's Hole, a valley south and west of the Tetons. After an eight-day journey, as they approached the village, Blue Feather could see that it was rather large for an Indian settlement, much larger, in fact, than they were led to believe.

When the villagers saw the party of ten riders and a single covered wagon approach, a stir went through the village and a large crowd of men, women, and children formed at the entrance to the village through which the travelers would come.

"Father, there must be more than a thousand people here, and look, now they are beginning to dance and cheer. They are gathering to celebrate your arrival!"

"No, Blue Feather, they are cheering not for me, but for the Lord, whom I represent. Let's not let the Lord be disappointed in our efforts to serve these people."

Fr. De Smet was led to the lodge of the great chief Tjolzshitsay who greeted him warmly.

"Father, we have prayed for the day that a black robe would visit our people and teach us the wisdom of the one true god, who created all things and reigns over all men. People of the Salish and the Pend d'Oreilles nations heard that you were coming and have been streaming here. We have more than 1,600 Indians visiting this village now, from various distinct tribes, including people who have traveled twenty-five days to be here!"

Fr. De Smet wiped a tear forming in his eye and said, "I am sorry that the Church did not send priests when first requested. Most priests are not cut out for such adventure, and I alone volunteered."

"Adventure?" The chief chuckled. "Indians are used to traveling great distances almost every moon! And frequently we must fight hostile tribes ourselves. But I do not blame your fellow priests for not wanting to leave their comfortable lives."

"Chief, I can stay at this village for a few days but then I must move on to the headwaters of the Missouri at Three Forks (in present-day Montana). While I am here, I will preach the word of God and baptize as many people as I can."

"Good, for many of the Salish nation are here. When the time comes, I will go with you, and you can baptize me and Chief Walking Bear of the Pend d'Oreilles in the waters of the great river. Our people will follow our example."

In the meantime, more of the Salish, Pend d'Oreilles, and Nez Perces migrated to this encampment. But this would be only a temporary location for these tribes and Fr. De Smet and Blue Feather discussed what the best course of action might be.

Blue Feather said, "Father, the traditional home of the Salish is quite a far distance from here. It's across the Divide in the Bitterroot Valley, at least a seven-day journey."

"Blue Feather, you have done God's work by serving as a translator for me and by teaching the children. They all seem to delight in the time you spend with them, and I am sure you planted the seed of faith and nurtured it with these little ones. But I think we have done as much as we can without additional priests and resources from the Jesuits. I propose that we return to St. Louis and present our case to the Jesuit leaders. And Blue Feather, you need to return to Winnie. I might never have been married, but I know a young woman doesn't want to feel abandoned by the man she loves."

Some days later, after some final lessons to the Indians and instructions to them to find a place to settle where a permanent mission might be established, Fr. De Smet, Blue Feather, and Kajicka began the journey back to St. Louis. Grigio, the huge wolf dog, still followed Fr. De Smet and happily walked with them.

As they began their trek, they were unaware that they were be-ing observed by Black Foot braves who were suspicious of the strange white man wearing black clothing who was traveling through what they considered their hunting grounds.

On occasion, Grigio would circle the wagon and the riders, looking attentively at the scenery around them. If something caught his eye, he stood still and stared in that direction as if deciding if there was any threat present. This became part of the wolf dog's routine, and the travelers took it seriously if Grigio be-came very still and stared in a certain direction for what seemed a long time.

As they approached a grove of trees, Grigio stood still, staring with ears up.

"Grigio, what do you see?" Blue Feather rode over to where Grigio was standing stone still. "I wonder what is out there."

They didn't have to wait long to find out as they pulled close to the grove of trees. Eight mounted Black Foot warriors charged at the travelers yelling war whoops. Father De Smet was driv-ing the wagon as one warrior swooped in and leaned in from his mount to swing a war club at the priest. Grigio was not going to let the priest get hurt. The wolf dog leaped up to the warrior and attached his teeth to the man's arm and pulled him to the ground. The horse became frightened and fled the scene while the wolf dog savagely attacked the Indian. Meanwhile, Blue Feather and Kajicka had dismounted and were shooting at their attackers who had dismounted and were trying to get close to their tar-gets so that they could count coop. It wasn't working. The two defenders quickly dropped four of the Black Foot warriors. This meant five attackers were down. The three unharmed warriors decided to kill the wolf dog with their arrows because the beast was perceived to be a magical entity protecting the shaman in the black robe. As they shot arrows at Grigio, he simply dodged them and ran after the attackers snarling. By now, thoroughly frightened by the powers of this wolf dog, the three remaining attackers were heard yelling, "It is a demon dog. This is evil medicine. There will be no defeating it." Then they decided to cut their losses and turned tail and ran.

The Indian warriors eventually found their horses and rode back to their encampment speaking of the white shaman in the black robe and his demon wolf dog. The story of this demon dog became embellished with each telling and the word spread to other bands of Black Foot Indians. Collectively, they decided to not harass this group of travelers again.

The trek home consumed four months and on December 31st Fr. De Smet was back again at St. Louis College. The Jesuits surrounded him and peppered him with questions about his adventure. The same was true for Blue Feather when he met with his classmates, most of whom had never ventured west of Westport.

Much to his dismay, the Society of Jesus lacked the resources for a new expedition and establishment of a permanent mission. Not taking no for an answer, Fr. De Smet embarked on a fundraising tour to Philadelphia, New York, and then down to New Orleans. When Mr. Mullanphy heard of the plan, he donated funds right away and even paid for Fr. De Smet's travel expenses, as well as expenses for Blue Feather and Winnie. As it turned out, Winnie had completed her midwifery course and was ready to return to St. Louis, so she would return with Blue Feather.

Fr. De Smet made good use of Blue Feather on this fund-raising tour. Probably a majority of Catholics in Philadelphia, New York, and other eastern cities that they visited had never met a "real-live Indian" before and were thrilled to hear him speak on how Indians lived in the far west and how they were open to the Gospel. Blue Feather benefited from the practice in public speaking. Audiences were held in rapt attention.

Once back home in St. Louis and after a visit to his family and Osage tribesmen, Blue Feather and Winnie settled in at the Mullanphy mansion at his invitation (insistence really). Settled again and back to college for Blue Feather, the young couple were independently thinking of matrimony. They were 19 years old -- not too young for marriage at all by the local mores and perhaps even kind of late for Indian marriages (girls typically married at 14 years of age).

One evening at the end of an after-dinner stroll, Blue Feather gently led Winnie to a park bench overlooking Chouteau's Pond. Dropping to one knee, Blue Feather took a deep breath and said, "Winnie, I can't imagine living without you. I want to spend the rest of my life with you as my wife. Will you marry me?

Winnie, with tears in her eyes, said, "Yes, of course I will! I want us to be together and never be separated."

The wedding took place at the Cathedral with Fr. De Smet officiating. Afterwards, Mr. Mullanphy held a reception for the young newlyweds at his mansion. Blue Feather's mother and grandfather attended as did several of the Chouteau relatives. Other guests came from the Osage village and St. Louis College. Winnie invited Mother Duchense and some girls from her days at the orphanage that she could find. Unfortunately, Winnie had no family members present.

Blue Feather and Winnie continued to live at the Mullanphy mansion and Mr. Mullanphy could not have been happier to have them stay with him. Blue Feather returned to full-time study at the college and Winnie apprenticed for an established midwife. The young couple was happy.

At the end of the spring semester of 1843 Blue Feather was ready to graduate with his A.B. (artium baccalaureus) with a concentration in linguistics. Then like any other freshly minted college graduate, he began to look for a position. Unfortunately, the economy was experiencing a depression[4] and jobs were hard to come by. After some months of searching for a position in vain, Mr. Mullanphy sat down with Blue Feather and said, "Son,

---

4. This was one of the longest and deepest depressions of the 19th century. It was a period of pronounced deflation and massive default on debt.) Employers weren't hiring.

I'm afraid that you are not going to find suitable work until the economy recovers. I've noticed how restless and unhappy you appear, like you are itching to get up and do something, build something and be productive. You have spent a great amount of your life out-of-doors, and I'll bet that you would rather be out there in the country and not stuck in this dirty old city. Have you thought of taking up farming as an occupation?"

"That was always Winnie's dream since she was 10 years of age! I know how to run a farm because I helped my grandfather on his farm and then also with the Jesuits at the seminary farm. But I don't have money to buy a farm, livestock, and the equipment needed to plant and harvest crops."

"Well, my boy -- I happen to know an old Irishman that would be happy to provide these things. I would buy the farm and you would work it for me. When it becomes productive enough to turn a profit, then you can start buying the property from me. Does that sound appealing to you, son? Oh, by the way, the land I'm thinking of buying adjoins the farm my nephew Shamus operates. I'll bet he'll want to help you raise your cabin and barn and dig a well. You don't have to accept my offer this minute, Blue Feather. What is it that Fr. De Smet always says? Oh, yes -- prayerfully consider this!"

"I'll talk this idea over with Winnie tonight! But I know one objection she will have (and I share this one) -- she would not want to live so far from you Mr. Mullanphy because you have been so kind and generous to us!"

"Well, lad, that would be sweet of her to say this. But I might want to move soon to a nice country home and leave city life behind. Shamus is saving an acre on his farm for me to build on. Have you noticed the terrible smells coming from the lake in recent months? Meat packers and factories have been building their horrible facilities on Chouteau's Pond and they are polluting both the air and the water. People are not using that lake for recreation the way they once did. I certainly don't blame them."

Winnie had no doubt in her mind that farm life was what she wanted; and so, in a matter of months, they moved to their new farm. Shamus and White Fawn were thrilled to have Blue Feather and Winnie as neighbors. For White Fawn, Winnie was a real godsend because there were not any other young women for miles around, and they soon became inseparable. Shamus helped Blue Feather build his log cabin and then recruited men from the local Catholic parish to help raise a barn.

White Fawn had already had her first child by Shamus, a boy they named Sean. But even after two years, there was no pregnancy for Winnie and Blue Feather. Back in those days, little was known about the causes of infertility. If a woman failed to conceive after repeated attempts, she was simply assumed to be barren, and few people thought of the husband as the source of the problem.

CHAPTER NINE

Shamus and Blue Feather had teamed up and won a contract as a supplier of vegetables to the U.S. Army at Jefferson Barracks south of St. Louis. On this particular day they were delivering two wagons loaded with vegetables and eggs. Their point of contact for the delivery was a young lieutenant Sam Grant who was serving as company quartermaster.

Blue Feather and Shamus started to unload their boxes of vegetables and eggs at the warehouse when young Lt. Grant rode up on a fine chestnut mare. It was obvious to Blue Feather that he was an excellent horseman and knew how to handle his steed.

As he dismounted, Sam Grant called over to Blue Feather and Shamus, "Fellows, you don't need to unload. I'll get some of my enlisted men to do that." Then he motioned over to a buck sergeant who gathered some helpers.

"Lieutenant, I noticed how well you ride a horse. I'm a little surprised the Army has you assigned to infantry and not cavalry," said Blue Feather.

"Thank you, sir for the compliment. As a matter of fact, I was widely recognized at West Point as one of the best horsemen in my class. But then, I was only average in academic subjects and in discipline. That ruled out the choicest assignments. And ironically, I can barely march in step. I have no sense of rhythm -- and I get assigned to infantry!"

Blue Feather gave a wry smile and said, "Well, Lieutenant as the Bible says "Whatever your work might be, do it as for the Lord and not for men. I'm sure your officers will recognize your talents if you keep producing."

"What are your names, fellows? I am Ulysses S. Grant, though my classmates decided to call me Uncle Sam Grant, and then shortened it to simply Sam."

"Good to make your acquaintance, Sam. I am Blue Feather Chouteau, and this is Shamus Mullanphy."

"Of the founding family of this city, may I ask?"

"Well, of the same family, but not a direct descendant of the founder."

"You appear to be an educated man, Blue Feather. Is that true?"

"Well, yes. I was educated by the Jesuits at their school for Indian boys in Florissant Missouri and then at St. Louis College."

"Is that a fact? By your name, I was thinking you might be at least part Indian. Have you mastered the traditional skills of an Indian brave? And do you know any Indian languages?"

At this point Shamus decided to speak for Blue Feather whom he thought was being too modest, "Lt. Grant, Blue Feather is a humble man. You might have to pry this information from him, but I'll tell you forthrightly, that he has all the skills of an Osage warrior, he speaks several Indian languages, and has made at least two trips west, serving as an interpreter for the Jesuit missionaries, and as a defender, protecting them from hostile Indians."

Sam Grant listened closely as Shamus spoke. "Blue Feather, the U.S. Army is in sore need of someone with your skills and experience."

Blue Feather and Shamus didn't say a word about their conversation with the young lieutenant when their families shared the evening meal later that same day. But Sam Grant was impressed so much with Blue Feather that he went to the company commander, Colonel Kearny, to discuss the promising young man he had found.

Colonel Kearny was with Captain Phillip St. George Cooke, the first commander of a new Army fort to be established in Central Texas, when Sam Grant was called into the office.

"Lt. Grant, you are aware that Captain Cooke here will be taking a company of cavalry and mounted infantry to central Texas to establish a fort -- soldiers are needed to protect wagon trains of settlers who are angering the Comanches, Apaches, and Kiowas for settling on their hunting grounds. These Indians are killing all adults, raping many of the women and girls, and sometimes taking the children captive. The Texas Rangers have been fighting these savages on their own, and they have won several victories over the Comanches, but their force is too small to be effective. We need the full force of the U.S. Army to contain this threat."

"The troops we have on hand to send on this expedition are mostly green, and practically none of them has traveled west of St. Louis. They haven't fought Indians before and don't know how to navigate across wide stretches of open prairie. So, we have a dire need of expert help -- if we send this company on this mission without expert help, they will surely die."

"That is why your note about this Blue Feather fellow was so interesting to me," said Colonel Kearny. "We need to see if we can entice Blue Feather to sign on as a U.S. Army scout."

"Blue Feather told me that the only thing that his wife ever really wanted was a real clapboard farmhouse, not a log cabin, and a farm where they can raise crops, have a herd of milk cows, and a variety of chickens. He seems quite committed to pleasing her, so I doubt that he could be easily won over to a job as a scout," said Sam Grant.

"So, she wants a nice farmhouse, does she? Lt. Grant, I want you to purchase the wood, nails, and tools needed to assemble a fine farmhouse. We will load up these materials on wagons and deliver it all to the Chouteau farm. You can have it charged to my personal account. Then I will offer Blue Feather a new home in exchange for say, 3 to 6 months of service as a scout for the U.S. Army. The Army will pay him a warrant officer's salary for his specialized skills and knowledge. And you know that this pay rate is lot better than even a sergeant's rate, so he won't be able to complain about compensation. I will also include carpenters, glaziers, roofers, and foundation layers from our enlisted staff. This will be an excellent training exercise for them. Let's see if this works!"

Sam Grant said, "Colonel, do you really have that kind of money to spend on a new house for a stranger?"

"As a matter of fact, Lieutenant, I do! My father was very wealthy. And I can't emphasize enough that Blue Feather is absolutely essential for this mission. Captain, you will be heading up this recruiting trip because Blue Feather will be reporting directly to you."

♋ ♋ ♋

When the wagons with building materials rolled up to the Chouteau farmhouse, Winnie was the first person to see them. Thoroughly confused and nervous over their unexpected arrival, Winnie rang the alarm bell that Blue Feather could hear out in the field and then hurry back to the farmhouse. Blue Feather arrived driving his buckboard wagon fairly hard. He was as confused as Winnie to see a half dozen freight wagons carrying building materials and a seventh wagon carrying enlisted men.

Blue Feather took his place by Winnie, as a soldier in an officer's uniform with captain's bars dismounted and walked up to them. The captain extended his hand in greeting. Blue Feather, warily shook it but only briefly before he said "Captain, why are you here? We have not done anything wrong, and we are exempt from removal to the Indian Territory."

"You are not in any trouble, Mr. Chouteau. I'm here because your country needs you. Shortly my company of soldiers will be traveling to Texas to establish a new fort for the purpose of protecting the thousands of Americans entering the state from the eastern and midwestern states. The Comanche, Apache, and probably the Kiowa have been attacking wagon trains and committing unspeakable crimes against the white settlers. And that is where your services are so desperately needed. I heard that you are something of a linguist and that you can speak Comanche, Apache, and Kiowa. We want peace with these people, but we cannot achieve peace without you, someone they can trust."

"Captain, there might be no reasoning or bargaining with the Comanches, whom I know the best. I have never dealt with the Apache before, but I don't expect that they will want to parley either."

"But you know their languages, right?"

"I'm almost fluent in Comanche and Kiowa, but not in Apache. But I can also communicate in sign language, which is the lingua franca of the western tribes."

"Mr. Chouteau, I am prepared to enlist you for a minimum of 90 days. Colonel Kearny wants to offer you the rank of warrant officer and a salary that is better than even the highest ranked sergeant is paid. Plus, as a type of signing bonus, he is offering you and your wife a new home for your farm, completely built and ready to take ownership. You will be gone for 90 days minimum, possibly longer."

Winnie's ears perked up at the mention of a new house. "How many bedrooms will this house have, and do you have any pictures I can look at?"

Blue Feather was a bit surprised by Winnie's interest and whispered to Winnie, "Winnie, we need to consider this offer carefully!"

"That's why I am looking over these plans carefully. Captain, could your men paint the house?

"Why yes, Mrs. Chouteau, in fact we have paint set aside for this purpose and we thought we would paint everything once we have the house all assembled."

"Of course, you'll be building a summer kitchen, right?"

"Yes, ma'am. We'll add that to the plans."

"Blue Feather, honey, I want this house!"

"But what about us being separated for three or more months? I thought you said you didn't want us ever to be separated again."

"Blue Feather, I know that you've been antsy these past months. I know you better than anyone. You need adventure -- I don't think you're well-suited for the simple life of a farmer, so if we can get ourselves a nice new home out of this, and a salary -- a good salary at that—for three months, I say go ahead and do this."

"But honey, you know that there will be some risk involved. We will be facing hostile Indians."

"You have faced hostile Indians before, and you've come out all right. You know how to fight and protect yourself. Besides, your country is calling you! This is important work. Perhaps not as important as being called by the Lord to translate and preach His word, but it is important work. So, I think you should go ahead and go on this mission."

"You know that you can't do this farm work on your own. I'll have to see if Shamus is willing to do it for some share of the income we would get from selling our produce and beef cattle."

White Fawn walked up and stood nearby and overheard their conversation, "Oh, I'm sure Shamus will be willing to help you out. I agree with Winnie. If you get a nice farmhouse for your efforts, that is what she always wanted."

"Since I was a little girl, and I told you this when we first met!"

"OK, I am persuaded. But good Lord, will I ever miss you, Winnie!"

"I will miss you too! You are the love of my life! But this is an opportunity for both of us. You'll get another taste of adventure, and I'll finally get my farmhouse."

After a handshake, the captain ordered his construction crew to begin work.

♋   ♋   ♋

Captain Cook had Blue Feather fitted for a warrant officer's uniform and swore him into the U.S. Army. Blue Feather had some misgivings still about joining the U.S. Army. After all, the Army had forced a migration of several eastern Indian tribes to Indian Territory, and the trip, known as the Trail of Tears, had a brutal effect on many people. But then Blue Feather thought that he might become a type of ambassador for the Indian nations within the U.S. Army and help Army officials become more just and merciful to Indians as they were forced to comply with federal policies. He decided that it was worth a try.

On the appointed day, Blue Feather reported for duty at Jefferson Barracks, near Saint Louis. As he became acquainted with the company of soldiers he was leading to Texas he discovered that they were mostly green enlisted men recruited from eastern cities. There were few veterans. As a unit they were not prepared for the long journey, and they had no idea what to expect if they were to fight hostile tribes such as the Comanches. Because of this, Blue Feather took on additional duties as an instructor, teaching the soldiers how the Comanches fought and how to best fight them. Even after three weeks of training Blue Feather felt that at most only one third of the troops were combat ready. He knew that he needed to speak to his superior officers.

He requested a meeting with Colonel Kearny through Captain Phillip St. George Cooke, and once he heard Blue Feather's proposal, he quickly set up a meeting with their commanding officer.

"All right, Mr. Chouteau, tell me your idea. Captain Cooke apparently thinks it is worth sticking out his neck for it."

"Yes, sir. My idea is to take a lesson learned from the recent Seminole War. The U.S. Army was losing to the Seminoles when their main weapon was the single shot Springfield. The Seminoles were able to concentrate their fire on soldiers reloading their weapons who at that point were basically defenseless. In later battles after the soldiers were then equipped with the

Colt revolvers, both pistols and rifles, they won their battles and eventually the war."

"Mr. Chouteau, I have read reports on these weapons and the consensus appears to be that they are fragile and far from ideal for the rugged conditions of war. So, if you are going to request that I outfit every man in my command with a repeating rifle, I will have to say no. However, I have read reports of the success of the Paterson Colt 5-shot revolver for the Texas Rangers fighting the Comanches; and so, if you want to try to secure such pistols for the men at the St. Louis Arsenal, I will sign the requisition papers.

Captain Cooke spoke up, "Colonel, I am assuming that the men have not had much practice with revolvers so I will make arrangements for training. Mr. Chouteau, I want you to work with our weapons trainers to prepare them for training one hundred soldiers on the use of these firearms."

"Yes, sir. I'll get right on it."

CHAPTER TEN

Three weeks later the company of soldiers left Jefferson Barracks headed southwest. Missouri was largely prairie turned farmland and rolling hills with cattle or milk cows grazing in the pastures. But the terrain became more rugged with steep hills and forest once they reached the Ozarks. They cut a course through the corner of Arkansas going as far south as Fort Smith where they replenished their supplies, and then they entered Indian Territory.

The company traveled in a southwesterly direction along what was known as the Texas, Shawnee, or Sedalia Trail which took them through the areas set aside for the Cherokee and Choctaw nations. For much of this journey Blue Feather and Captain Cooke rode next to each other and naturally discussed topics of mutual interest. Captain Cooke, a West Point graduate, was pleased to have another educated man in his company.

"Mr. Chouteau, if you look through your field glasses at two o'clock, you'll see where something of the old South has been imported here."

Spotting the place the captain had been indicating, Blue Feather exclaimed, "Why, it looks like a mansion you would find on a Southern plantation! Here? In Indian Territory?"

"Yes, indeed! Some of the Cherokee families transported here were wealthy landowners in North Carolina. Now, look again out in the fields."

"There are Negro farm hands, and it appears that there are no Indian workers."

"Those Negroes are slaves. When the Cherokee were moved here in 1835, they had 1,500 black slaves. Today the number is more like 4,000."

"I was born and raised in Leesburg, a small city in Virginia about 30 miles west of Washington City. Growing up in the South, I saw many plantations and many slaves. I have always been opposed to slavery, and if a civil war ever breaks out between the Northern states where all men are free and the Southern states where some men are slaves, I will fight on the side of the North."

"Let's hope and pray that slavery can be abolished in a peaceful way, through legislation."

"Amen to that!"

A couple of hours passed, and Blue Feather was first to notice four men on horseback blocking the trail.

"This could be trouble ahead, Captain."

"I think I know what they are up to. They don't pose any threat to us, but it looks like the colored man has his arms tied behind his back."

As they drew closer to the riders blocking the trail, they noticed that the black man was gagged with a dark rag. The apparent leader of the group was a grizzled white man with the remnants of a cigar stuck in his mouth.

"Howdy, Captain! I'm Jimmy Edwards, and my companions are Billy Wilson, and Donny McBiden. We are a posse deputized by the Cherokee Nation to capture slaves who have done run away from their rightful owners. We're taking back this here nigger to his master. Have you seen any niggers runnin loose in your travels?"

At the mention of slaves, the black man shook his head back and forth vigorously and somehow was able to spit out his gag. With pleading eyes, the man blurted out, "Captain, these men are lying! I am a free man, and I can prove it!"

"Shut up, nigger! You ain't got permission to talk. Captain, this darkie did not have any papers with him, and he fits the description of a runaway slave."

"That's a lie, you took my paper and you tore it up."

That accusation earned the black man a knot on his head when one of his captors struck him hard with the barrel of his revolver.

The captain then spoke, "Now, let me tell you what I think is going on here. I think you're telling the truth when you say you've been deputized to capture and return runaway slaves. But I think that you're also capturing any black man or woman, slave or free, that you can and selling them to the highest bidder in Arkansas. In the case of this free man, you have committed the crimes of kidnapping, assault and battery, and selling him when he is not your property. You get a lot more money selling him to a slave dealer in Arkansas than you would in a reward from a grateful slave owner."

"Young man, where were you going when you were accosted?"

"Captain, I was going to Mexico. A country that freed its slaves in 1829."

"Mr. Chouteau -- untie this man and bring him to our quartermaster and get him outfitted with some food items for his trip. Sergeant Major Timmins and Corporal Riley, keep your guns on these criminals while their former prisoner is set free."

"Captain, you've no right to take this nigger from us!"

"I have every right to stop this crime and free this man from your clutches! You should be ashamed of yourself. There is no honor in what you are doing. I should arrest you and your henchmen and deliver you to Fort Smith, where you can be tried in a court of law."

Jimmy Edwards stared at the captain and shook with rage, then suddenly he drew his gun and cocked it. Then BAM! His pistol went flying out of his hand along with a few fingers. Before Edwards could shoot the captain, Blue Feather had drawn his gun and shot the gun out of Edwards's hand.

The slave hunter was now screaming over his misfortune and looking at his mangled hand dripping blood rather profusely.

"Our company does not yet have a medical doctor, but we will bandage your hand. Private Fitzsimmons, bring our medical kit to the front and bandage this man's hand!"

After Edwards's hand was bandaged, Captain Cooke called over to the posse as they departed, "You should get a doctor to tend to your wound. There's one at Fort Smith who would be able to help you."

Edwards frowned and snarled out, "If I see any of you in this neck of the woods, I'll shoot your hands off or something worse!"

The captain simply waved them off and turned away.

"Well, Mr. Chouteau, we lost a good hour of daylight bickering with that fool. I appreciate your handiness with the gun. Your preemptive strike might have saved my life."

"I was simply in the right place at the right time. I didn't know I could react that quickly and not take a wild shot. I've never practiced the quick draw, but maybe I should -- it could come in handy."

"Now, tell me the truth -- were you aiming for his hand?"

Chuckling, "Honestly...no! I know enough to aim for a large target. In this case it was his torso. But my shot was off by about a foot. Maybe the Lord wanted this man to live long enough to repent."

"Well, I would not bank on that!"

♋ ♋ ♋

The wagon train was about 20 miles north of Fredericksburg, Texas when they encountered a company of Texas Rangers headed in the opposite direction.

"Greetings Captain! I am Captain Jack Hays of the Texas Rangers. What brings you to Texas?"

"Pleased to meet you, Captain. I am Captain Phillip St. George Cooke. This company of soldiers is here to erect new buildings and fortifications for Camp Houston, then we will be deployed at Camp Houston to temporarily augment the company of soldiers already there until another company deploys there for the long-term."

"Then we will be working together because protecting farmers and travelers from the depredations of the Comanche and Kiowa is our primary mission. We were fixing to climb to the top of this here hill, called Bear Mountain by the locals, to reconnoiter the area. You can see for miles around from the top of that mount."

"I'll send my scout, Mr. Chouteau, with you."

At the top of Bear Mountain, the Rangers and Blue Feather saw in the distance a large party of Indians headed in a northeasterly direction toward Fredericksburg.

"Scheiss! They are headed straight for Fredericksburg" exclaimed a blonde-haired Ranger with a German accent.

"Do you have any Rangers in town or soldiers?" asked Blue Feather.

"Nein, not much to speak of. Most of us were on this patrol."

"Then we need to get there before those Indians get there! I doubt they have a peaceful trading mission in mind. Let's go report this right away!" said Blue Feather.

Blue Feather and the Ranger scouts descended the hill as quick as they safely could and reported to their captains.

"Captain Hays, Captain Cooke! There is a large band of Indians riding toward Fredericksburg from the southwest!"

"Any idea of how many?" asked Captain Cooke.

"I think there are between 70 and 80 braves. They are riding fairly hard and so I don't think that they have friendly intentions," responded Blue Feather.

"Then Rangers, let's get down to Fredericksburg before this war party!" Captain Hays shouted waving his arm.

"Captain, we can't move as fast as you with these wagons, but we'll double-time it to get to the town and be your backup," said Captain Cooke.

"It will be greatly appreciated, I assure you!"

With that, the Rangers began their gallop into the town.

Captain Cooke, turned to the sergeant major, "Pass the word down the line. Be sure your weapon is loaded because it looks like we're going to fight!"

The Rangers were successful in getting to the town first and getting set for the attack. This meant getting townspeople off the streets and setting up barricades at the entrances to the town. Civilians who had weapons weren't discouraged from manning some of the barricades and some took positions on the roofs of buildings.

When the Indians (who turned out to be Comanche, as expected) arrived, they had to adjust their plans for a quick victory. But they looked upon the situation as a challenge. The main street in Fredericksburg was extra wide so that large freight wagons could turn around. That gave the Indians enough space to swoop in, fire a few arrows or bullets if they had them, and then reverse course. Then they noticed the Army caravan in the distance. The war chief dispatched twenty or so of his braves to attack the wagon train thinking these would be worth looting.

Blue Feather noticed the smaller war party heading their way and yelled "Circle the wagons!"

The men barely got the wagons in the right configuration when the Comanches attacked. Fighting was fierce, with the soldiers having the advantage of the large freighter wagons serving as cover. But even with the advantage of cover, some of the soldiers experienced a paralyzing fear, and some, if they were not overcome by fear, exposed too much of themselves. Five soldiers were killed but even more Comanches were killed. But as is the practice with the Comanche, if they determine the cost of winning is too high, they break off and retreat. Live and fight another day.

"Will that be the last we see of them today, Mr. Chouteau?" asked Captain Cooke.

"No, sir. I expect them to return under the cover of darkness to retrieve their fallen warriors. If we or the Rangers post guards, we might witness their return."

"Well, we won't interfere with that, but I think posting guards would be prudent! How many Comanches did we kill?"

"I counted eight bodies, sir. One brave might have still been alive but severely wounded. That was about one-tenth of their war band."

Later Captains Hays and Cooke discussed the situation with the Comanches.

"Captain Hays, I'm torn between two obligations. The first being the defense of this town and its civilian population, and the second being the moving on to Camp Houston (which will become Fort Martin Scott) to fortify it and deploy these men there temporarily while a company of dragoons (mounted infantry) arrive for long term deployment."

"Captain Cooke, I appreciate your situation. Listen, I think that the Comanches will be licking their wounds a couple of days and then return with a larger force. I'll request that you remain with us for three days to reinforce our defenses."

"Captain Hays, I can grant that request. The only reservation I have is whether the Comanches will wait until they see the U.S. Army leaving before they attack again."

"Well, tell you what -- we can have ready a large pile of firewood that once set afire would send up a large column of smoke. That will be your signal to return to Fredericksburg to fend off a Comanche attack. You will be only a few miles away."

"Excellent, then I will have my troops set up camp wherever you indicate!"

Blue Feather had soldiers posted on rooftops of buildings to surveille the countryside for any sign of an Indian attack. It was early on the third day that the Comanches attacked again. The soldiers serving as lookouts could see smoke rising in the distance at a couple of places some miles northwest of the city. These were the burning farmhouses that families had abandoned in fleeing ahead of the Indian attacks.

The town of Fredericksburg now had swollen in population by a hundred people, including men, women, and children. Local churches were turned into refugee housing for these displaced persons.

The Comanches attacked around 9:00 in the morning. Blue Feather had estimated their number at about 110 braves. Most were armed with bow and arrow, lances, and tomahawks; but a few had rifles stolen from farmhouses they had ransacked and then destroyed.

Knowing how much white people valued their homes, the Comanches tried to set several homes in the town ablaze with flaming arrows. This proved to be a great diversionary tactic since armed townspeople, if not rangers or soldiers, would race to extinguish the fire. This made the battle all the more difficult for the still green troops who hailed primarily from the eastern states. But fortunately, a party of six buffalo hunters happened to be staying in town. They volunteered their services to Blue Feather.

"We was lookin for one of them captains to volunteer our Hawkens rifles to the defense of this here town. If we kin get up on a roof top or two, we kin shoot them Injuns right off their horses while they are still hundreds of yards away!"

"That's a great idea! That might turn this battle around. Run over to the general store and get yourselves some ladders if you need them. If the storekeeper tries to stop you, tell him that Warrant Officer Chouteau directed you do so."

After a quick nod, the six hunters ran off. Minutes later Blue Feather could see them climbing their ladders, and minutes after that, he could hear their powerful rifles fire .50 caliber rounds at targets sometimes three or four hundred yards in the distance. One of their shots killed the Comanche war chief, causing great confusion. As their horses wheeled about, two more chiefs were killed. On another rooftop, two of the snipers chose to target braves carrying torches and braves preparing to shoot flaming arrows. Witnessing their fellow warriors fall dead, hearing a loud shot, but not even seeing the shooter, the Comanches abandoned their arson and retreated to what they thought was a safe distance. But apparently, it wasn't far enough, because two more warriors were shot from their horses. Before they got their wits about them, the Comanches lost another six warriors to the long-range snipers. Their total losses now numbering 21 warriors, the Comanches decided to retreat and fight another day.

After the Comanches' retreat, Captain Cooke caught up to Blue Feather and said, "Mr. Chouteau, I heard that you encouraged those buffalo hunters to serve as snipers with their long-range buffalo guns. I'm glad you did because their shooting saved the day for us. What rifle were they using, do you know?"

"Yes sir, they were using Hawkens rifles which fires a .50 caliber round. The rifle is handmade in St. Louis."

"We surely could use more of those rifles in the U.S. Army! I'm going to requisition some of these Hawkens. I doubt that the Army will approve my purchase request, but I'll plead my case to Colonel Kearny who might have enough influence to make this possible."

Just then Captain Hays walked up and entered the conversation. "Captain, I overheard you say you wanted to get some of those Hawkens rifles for your soldiers. I'm thinking of offering positions in the Texas Rangers to these buffalo hunters. I can't match the income they might make from buffalo hides, but I can pay them a regular salary, and pay for room and board at the hotel. Beats living in a musty old tent and sleeping on the hard ground!"

After the battle Captain Cooke mustered his troops and they prepared to continue their journey to Camp Houston. Once there, they would begin building a stockade and then a larger barracks for the troops. The officers' offices and living quarters would be constructed last.

Blue Feather's ninety days were almost complete, and he was itching to return home. Construction on the stockade was progressing slowly with sections in adobe and others in stone and the camp was gradually becoming more secure with at least low unfinished walls surrounding the parade grounds. The soldiers felt like they would be safer now, at least in the camp, but Blue Feather advised the captain that the men should be wearing side arms because they were still susceptible to Comanche attacks.

"Don't let your guard down", counseled Blue Feather, "We should be like the men rebuilding the wall of Jerusalem under Nehemiah, keeping our weapons at the ready while we work."

Captain Cooke called over his Master Sergeant and ordered him to have the men combat ready even as they worked construction.

The work of building the wall involved setting large stones on each other and using mud as mortar and when the stones ran out, the men turned to adobe to finish the remainder of the palisade. A strong gate was made of thick wood.

A company of dragoons arrived some days ahead of schedule to deploy at the fort, now renamed Fort Martin Scott after a hero in the war with Mexico. The evening of their arrival the officers had supper together at the Officer's mess. The table conversation turned to news from back east.

"Well, Captain Cooke, the most significant news happened in our mutual hometown, Saint Louis. A terrible pestilence, a cholera epidemic, was working its way through the city full swing when we left Jefferson Barracks on May 20th. Authorities expect that 10 percent of the population will die before this epidemic runs its course. But then another tragedy struck on May 17th when a steamboat caught fire, burned through its moorings and drifted into another steamboat and set it afire. Eventually the fire spread to dozens of other steamboats, and eventually to warehouses and then the business district and to an old residential area nearby."

As Blue Feather listened to this news, he grew increasingly anxious.

The next morning Blue Feather was in Captain Cooke's office to ask for his release from his ninety-day period of service. He didn't say this, but if he wasn't released, he would simply have to go absent without leave.

Captain Cooke listened carefully to Blue Feather's request then said, "I will approve your request for leave, Mr. Chouteau, but first I must know if you intend to resign your position with the U.S. Army."

"Captain, that depends on what I find when I return to my farm in Missouri. If Winnie needs me, I should probably resign and resume farming."

"Mr. Chouteau, you are a fine officer and soldier. I would be sad to lose you. But you have family obligations, I understand. Go home to your wife and make sure all is well back at the farm."

"Thank you, sir. I will be leaving at first light tomorrow."

The captain seemed a bit surprised but recovered and simply nodded.

At first light, Blue Feather readied his horse, collected his few belongings, and packed them up, and made sure his weapons were loaded. The U.S. Army carbine was put into its scabbard and his side arm into its holster. He also had a bow and quiver of arrows. As he led his horse out of the stable, he was surprised to see most of the soldiers he had served with walking up to him and wishing him well.

Blue Feather planned on riding his horse, a fine chestnut, at a quick lope until one of them grew too tired to move on. Their route would head in a northeasterly direction and multiple rivers and streams would be crossed. As the sun set on the third day of his ride, Blue Feather smelled food cooking. It had a foreign aroma.

Unconsciously, he had slowed down to a trot, thinking about the food. And now he was able to see a large bonfire in the center of a village and various smaller cooking fires through a copse of pine trees. Without warning, a burly brave ran up from behind and struck him hard with a war club. Blue Feather fell from his horse stunned, giving three warriors from the village the opportunity to tie him up and drag him into the village.

In and out of consciousness, as he was being dragged into the village, he could see his attackers were short thick men, heavily tattooed, with mohawk-like haircuts. Rather than teepees, longhouses, or earthen lodges this tribe built large cylindrical homes. Blue Feather was tied to a post and then an older man stooped down to talk with him.

The man said, "I am Caddi Nacogdoches of the Caddo nation. I am the chief of this village. You are an Army scout sent to spy on us. You were going to estimate our strength and report to your commanding officer. I will tell you this, spy, this Caddo village will not move. We will not be forced to move north to the Indian Territory, to some land forsaken by the gods."

"Chief you are correct in saying that I am an Army scout, but I am not a spy. I led a company of soldiers to establish a new fort near Fredericksburg to help defend the settlers from the Comanches. My enlistment period has ended, and I am trying to return to my farm in Missouri."

"You appear to be an Indian, yet you wear the uniform of the white soldiers? Are you a traitor to your own people?"

"My name is Blue Feather Chouteau. I am half Indian – my mother belongs to the Osage nation and my father was

French-American. I have spent much of my life with both the whites and the Indians. I am loyal to both and seek only peace and friendship between all nations of people."

"Friendship between all nations? You lie! You are here to spy on us so your commanding officer can send in an overwhelming force, defeat us, and march the survivors to the Indian Territory."

"No, I told you I was passing through on my way back to Missouri. That is the truth, so help me God."

"A few years ago, your horse soldiers could have been friends to us and defend us against those dogs the Comanches. But they didn't. You know what I think? The Army just wanted us Indians to kill off each other. So, don't talk to me about friendship and peace!"

"Chief Nacogdoches, I believe him! Please don't harm him. I looked through his pack. He has books, like the Bible, and notebooks where he has written down the tongues of several Indian nations. He is not a spy, he is a scholar, a wise man. He's not here to do us any harm."

The speaker was a young white girl about 16 or 17 years old, a pretty brunette with blue eyes.

"You see this girl? Her name is Louise Marie. We rescued her from the Comanches who had killed her parents when they came this way to settle in Texas. We can be a friend to the white people. Now, why do you try to learn all these Indian languages? Are you planning to trick them into moving to the Indian Territory?"

"No, my goal, which I have had since I was thirteen is to someday open a school for Indian children of all tribes. These children would be prepared to assume leadership roles in their tribes. I figure that if we can learn something of each other's languages, beliefs, and customs we can promote peace among the tribes, and you would not have to worry about defending yourselves from Comanches, Kiowa, or any other tribe."

"Ha! You really are a dreamer! But I think I like you and I see that you are what you say you are and are harmless to the Caddo people."

"Then please untie me and I'll be on my way!"

"Not so fast! I want to wait and see if some horse soldiers come looking for you. If no one comes looking for you by tomorrow morning, I'll send you on your way. Besides, it is sunset now and you should rest yourself and your horse and have some food. Louise Marie, go fetch Blue Feather some food."

"Yes, Chief Nacogdoches."

Minutes later Louise Marie returned, carrying two bowls of some sort of stew. She set the bowls down and untied him so that he could eat.

"Sir, you said your name was Blue Feather Chouteau – are you from Saint Louis? The Chouteau family founded Saint Louis."

"Yes, I am. How did you know of the Chouteau family?"

"My name is Louise Marie Blanchette and I lived in Saint Charles with my parents. We were familiar with some families in Saint Louis, even visiting them on occasion. I left Saint Charles with my parents about four years ago."

"Then your family joined a wagon train headed to Texas?"

"Yes, and we weren't in this country long, just a few days into it, when the Comanches attacked us and killed everyone except me." She paused a moment, tearing up and sniffling.

"Then a young warrior raped me. I was just 13 years old and had never been with a man before. Now, no respectable white man will want me if they find out I am no longer a virgin. In fact, no Caddo man wants me either because I was with a Comanche."

"Louise Marie, I think we need to return you to Saint Charles. Do you still have family there?"

"Yes! I have an aunt and uncle who would take me in."

"Then I must find a way to get the Chief to release you so that you might return with me to Missouri."

After some moments of silence Louise Marie looked at him timidly and said, "I know a way."

"Surprised, Blue Feather said, "What way is that?"

"If you marry me, you can take me with you to Missouri. Caddo men return to their own band or village with their new bride."

Blue Feather was speechless for a couple of seconds and then said, "But Louise Marie, I am already married!"

"I was thinking that you were, but the Chief doesn't know about your wife, does he?"

"No, I did not mention my wife."

"Then let's not tell him. Let's be married according to the Caddo custom and then you can take me home with you.

"Louise Marie, this would be a terrible deception. I am Catholic and I would be sinning before God."

"As would I! I am Catholic like you. But I don't see another way."

"Will the chief allow you to marry me?"

"He will be eager to see me go, since I am a burden to him now with no other prospect of marriage."

"I must think and pray about this idea. We can talk in the morning."

The morning came after a night of soul searching and prayer. Blue Feather had decided that the best course of action was to marry Louise Marie so that she could return to Missouri with him. When he met Louise Marie he said, "I've decided to go ahead with your plan."

Louise Marie smiled and hugged him and said, "Then over the next couple of days we need to make a good show of falling in love. The Caddo don't necessarily marry for love, but the chief knows white people usually do. So, it must look like we are falling in love."

"I think I can be convincing", Blue Feather said, then blushing when he realized what he said.

Louise Marie smiled and said, "Me too! Then she hugged him again and kissed him on his mouth.

Shortly after Louise Marie left him alone to do her chores, Chief Nacogdoches walked up to Blue Feather and said, "Young man, I can see that our adopted daughter has grown very fond of you! Are you also fond of her?"

"Yes, I am. She is a very delightful young woman."

"You know that she is old enough to marry, don't you?"

"Yes, Chief."

"Then you should know that a Comanche dog raped her before we could rescue her. That ruins her chances of marrying a white man. Even our Caddo braves will not touch her."

"She was just a young girl of 13 when she was raped. It was no fault of her own. She will make a fine wife and mother."

"Yes, then keep that in mind." Then the chief walked away.

If he were going to spend a few days in this Caddo village, Blue Feather thought it would be a good use of his time to record their language. Seeing the chief later in the day, he asked,

"Chief Nacogdoches, you heard that I have transcribed the spoken languages of several Indian tribes into a written form. With your permission I would like to do that with the Caddo language. It would involve sitting down with various villagers who speak some English or French and getting them to speak the names of common objects and animals and speak to me in simple sentences so that I can get a sense of Caddo grammar."

The Chief's eyes widened, and he fell silent for a couple seconds. "That would be acceptable, I trust that you will only use this knowledge for good. I will have Louise Marie help you find willing villagers."

"Thank you, Chief Nacogdoches."

Blue Feather and Louise Marie worked closely together for a week and became increasingly fond of each other. They ate together and bathed together at the Boykin Creek, but slept separately. When Blue Feather had finished his work transcribing the

Caddo language, which he had found to be related to the Pawnee language, he and Louise Marie went to the Chief to ask his permission to marry.

The Chief smiled and said, "I was wondering what took you so long. Of course, you should marry. But you cannot settle here, you must go to the village of the husband. The wedding will take place tonight. Fortunately, the high priest (the Xinesi) is visiting our Hassinai group of Caddo Indians. We will hold the ceremony tonight at sundown on the sacred mound."

The wedding took place on top of a man-made mound with a tall conical building at its center. The whole village turned out for the wedding, and afterwards there was a wedding feast held in their honor. Then the time came for the couple to be led to the wedding hut, a smaller version of the large conical structures the Caddo used as homes. Inside there was a woven grass mat for flooring and a bed and chairs. The Caddo were unusual among the Indian tribes in having such items in their homes.

Blue Feather sat down heavily on the bed and was startled to hear tinkling noises coming from underneath the bed. "What was that sound?" Louise Marie answered, "Those are seashells and potsherds strung to the underside of the bed. The couple's lovemaking makes this sound ring out. It entertains the villagers outside surrounding our wedding bed. It's part of the festivities."

Blue Feather gulped and wondered what he had got himself into. While he was still contemplating this matter, Louise Marie undressed. Blue Feather could see by the candlelight that she was indeed beautiful, and his body reacted strongly to this stimulation.

His desire for this young woman temporarily overwhelmed his loyalty to Winnie and he gave in to his desire. The seashells and potsherds made quite a racket and then grew quiet. At that point he and Louise Marie could hear the women and girls giggling outside. It had been very entertaining to them, and they went home happy for the newlyweds.

The next morning Blue Feather woke up and watched Louise Marie get out of bed and put her clothing back on. He remembered then what had happened, and he began to feel profound guilt. *Oh, what have I done dear God?*

Louise Marie was quiet that morning and felt the pang of guilt when she noticed Blue Feather's distress. *Forgive me dear Lord, for I have tempted him beyond his ability to remain true to his marriage vows.*

They ate that morning in near silence and with minimal eye contact. When he finished, Blue Feather said, "Louise Marie, please gather your belongings and say your farewells. We should get on the trail in the next hour. I will get my US Army equipment, personal belongings, and saddle from the Chief and bring our horses back here all ready to go. The Chief has given you a mule you called Evangeline for the journey."

"Yes, she was one of the mules pulling my parents' covered wagon. She is gentle to riders."

Blue Feather looked up and saw that the Chief was standing there. "There's no need to go look for me, here I am. Your horse is already saddled. And here are your other belongings. Louise Marie, I can see that you are sad because you must leave us. But believe me, this is for the best. You have a fine husband now and you can return to Missouri and live among your own people."

"Yes, of course Chief. I want to thank you again for rescuing me from the Comanche. Without you, I would have spent the rest of my life wishing I were dead."

"And Blue Feather, I will pray to the Great Spirit that you and Louise Marie will be safe on your long journey home. How many days will your journey require?"

"Chief, I figure about 21 days but that would require eight hours per day in the saddle."

Louise Marie almost grimaced at this thought, because now she was remembering the journey she made to Texas with her parents four years ago.

The chief said, "Young bride, I saw the momentary fear in your eyes when you thought of riding a mule for eight hours a day. I will give you an additional mule, Cosette; then you will have two mules to pull a buckboard wagon, if you find you need one. Come to think of it, Louise Marie, Evangeline and Cosette belonged to your parents, so I am simply returning to you what is rightfully yours through inheritance."

Louise Marie made a point of capturing Blue Feather's attention, "Husband, we will need a buckboard wagon! Can you afford one?"

Blue Feather almost smiled despite his downcast spirit and said, "I have my wages from the U.S. Army, so yes, we can afford one. We'll look for one in the next big town we encounter on the trail."

Very few words were spoken for the first few hours of their journey. Then they stopped for a brief rest and mid-day meal. Louise Marie spoke first, "Blue Feather, I want to say that I am sorry for causing you to sin last night. I'm not sure why I was so bold and offered you myself by disrobing in front of you. Perhaps I just wanted to be really married and I was living out a fantasy."

"Louise Marie, you didn't cause me to sin. I saw you and wanted you, and I gave in to my temptation. I broke my wedding vows and committed adultery with you. I was unfaithful to my wife."

"You must have gone several months without the attentions of your wife. I won't offer that as an excuse, but I could sense a tremendous need in you, and I took advantage of you."

"Yes, the need was real, but my needs should be secondary to my duty to God. I failed Him. Well, I won't fail again. For the remainder of this journey, we've got to be chaste."

"Blue Feather, I want you to know that I thought I was in love with you, but I will not act on that feeling again by tempting you, out of respect for your marriage."

Blue Feather hesitated a moment but then said, "And I was strongly attracted to you as well. But last night I just let myself get carried away. My foremost commitment is to Winnie – I must always remember this!"

They continued their journey cutting east to Fort Smith in Arkansas. There they sought out a dealer of wagons and finding a used covered wagon to their liking, they purchased it for $100. It was not a cheap, low-end model, nor was it a high-end model. It was manufactured by Studebaker and was in good condition.

"I thought you were going to buy a buckboard wagon."

"I thought that you might be more comfortable traveling and sleeping in a covered wagon."

"Oh, that's very considerate of you," and she hugged him and kissed him on the cheek.

"That was just a friendly kiss to say thank you," she said with some embarrassment.

"That's OK. The next thing we need to do is drive over to the army fort so that I can get my wages from the paymaster."

Blue Feather was wearing his Army uniform when he visited the fort. He found the paymaster's window in the headquarters building. The paymaster looked up from his desk as Blue Feather stepped up to the window. "You are not stationed at this fort, are you? Well, what can I do for you?

"Has the courier with the payroll for Camp Houston left yet?"

"No, not yet. What is your name?"

"I am Warrant Officer Blue Feather Chouteau."

"Checking my list here...yes, I can give you your pay. Oh, and here is a letter that came for you yesterday."

"Thank you", Blue Feather said receiving his pay and letter.

Back at the covered wagon, Louise Marie was standing and stretching herself, thinking of the next leg of their trek.

"Did you get a letter from home as well as your pay?"

"Yes, appears so."

"Here let me hold it and I can read it to you as you drive if you want me to. But I'll have to read it to myself first because I haven't read anything in pert near four years."

"Well, I guess that would be fine. Go ahead please."

"The letter is from a mister Shamus Mullanphy in Saint Peter's Missouri. Oh, that's real close to Saint Charles."

"Yes, it is. Shamus and I have adjoining farms. While I was away, he was taking care of things for me and watching over my wife Winnie."

"He sounds like a true friend."

"That he is, and his wife, White Fawn, as well.

"Oh, it's good that Winnie had another woman as a friend close by."

"Yes, we were pretty close all right, we could look out our window and see their house not more than 50 yards away."

"OK, let me see what is in this letter. I'll read it through silently first, so I don't stumble on any words when I read aloud to you."

Blue Feather just nodded and kept looking straight ahead.

The letter had much more significance than Louise Marie could have imagined.

Dear Blue Feather,

I write this letter with such a heavy heart. It seems that it was God's will to take your precious Winnie from this life and bring her into eternal life in heaven. White Fawn and I are so sorry. White Fawn has cried inconsolably for days now, she mourns her closest friend so.

Winnie fell victim to the cholera epidemic in Saint Louis. She had gone to Saint Louis when she heard that old Patrick had taken seriously ill, not with cholera, but with a cancer. Winnie, being the lovely soul that she was, went to minister to him as a nurse at his sister's home in the colored neighborhood of the city. Little did she know, none of us knew really, how contagious that terrible cholera disease was. Word of her illness got to my uncle, John Mullanphy, and he personally came to take Winnie to his mansion where she might be more comfortable. And she did rest better in her nice bedroom in the servants' quarters for one night. But the next night, she died in her sleep. Uncle John had tried to stay with her, to care for her. But it was not meant to be. Uncle John, himself, came down with the disease, and he died two days later. Winnie is buried in the Mullanphy family plot at the Catholic cemetery.

I am so very sorry, Blue Feather, my dear friend. White Fawn and I will be praying for you in this time of grief. We will be here to help you in any way that we can.

Most sincerely yours,

Shamus

Blue Feather looked over at Louise Marie and he noticed that her eyes were getting teary, and now tears were flowing down her cheek. "Oh, Blue Feather, it is terrible news. I can read it to you, but it might be better if you pulled over."

Blue Feather looked at Louise Marie and stopped the wagon. Then he extended his hand for the letter and said, "Here, let me read the letter myself."

He stepped down from the wagon and read the letter silently. Then he said, "Oh my precious Winnie...I can't believe this...how can this be happening?" Then a wave of crushing grief fell over him and he stumbled to his knees, then sprawled face down on the ground.

Beating the ground with his fist he cried, "Why Father, why? Why would you take her from me? Did I do something to offend you, dear God?" Then it dawned on him, and another spasm of grief shook his person, "Oh my God, was it because I broke my vows and was unfaithful to Winnie? Oh, dear God, no!"

Louise Marie had stepped down and was kneeling next to the prone Blue Feather, but she hesitated to touch him or try to console him. Finally, she said, "Blue Feather, if you want to lie down in the bed of the wagon for a while, I can drive the wagon."

Blue Feather sat up and was beginning to pull himself together. Embarrassed by his tears, he didn't look at Louise Marie but said, "I will ride my own horse for a spell. I'll never leave you entirely alone – I'll just be a shout away."

"OK, Blue Feather. That sounds fine. I'll shout if I need help."

Blue Feather nodded and mounted his horse and rode some 50 yards ahead of Louise Marie and the wagon. Left alone with his horse, Blue Feather continued to grieve. Eventually, Blue Feather drifted back to Louise Marie, "We should find a place to set camp soon. I smell water perhaps a quarter mile ahead. That is where we'll set up camp."

"Good, I bought a small smoked ham in Fort Smith. I'll heat some up for our dinner. I also have some chicory coffee and hardtack biscuits."

They found a good place to camp near a stream. Blue Feather took care of the animals and Louise Marie made a cooking fire and prepared the meal.

They were silent during the meal, with Blue Feather gazing deeply into his chicory. Louise Marie thought *Oh this poor troubled soul! And to think, I was the cause of his sin – I tempted him beyond his control, and he thinks that God has punished him!* At the same time, Blue Feather was thinking *It was my weakness of character, my turning of my back to God, that led me to sin; it was not Louise Marie's fault. But why Lord, did you punish Winnie as well as me?*

That night Blue Feather laid out his bedroll under the wagon, while Louise Marie slept inside. Around midnight it started to rain, first gently, then torrentially. At first Blue Feather tried to ignore the situation, but then he grabbed his bedroll and climbed inside the covered wagon which had a nearly weather-proof canvas top. Louise Marie woke as Blue Feather laid his bedroll next to hers. He noticed her sitting up and said, "It's raining too hard to sleep under the wagon."

She said, "It's OK, you are welcome to sleep here."

He fell asleep and slept soundly until he felt a drip strike his thick hair. Instinctively, he rolled to his side, and forgetting where he was and who he was with, he reached over to pull over Louise Marie to cuddle. She woke at his touch, but realizing that he was sleeping, she made no attempt to extract herself.

A couple of hours passed, and Louise Marie woke again and noticed Blue Feather had left the wagon. Looking out the opening, she could see Blue Feather with a lantern at his feet leaning against a tree. His whole body appeared to shake with his silent sobs.

Louise Marie thought, *Oh Lord, if only Blue Feather could come to love me as he loved Winnie!*

CHAPTER ELEVEN

During the remainder of their trek to Saint Charles, Blue Feather seemed to be working through his grief and he spoke more. "Have you thought what you will do when you find your aunt and uncle in Saint Charles? Will they send you to school, or will you find a job?"

"My uncle had a prosperous haberdashery in downtime Saint Charles, so I doubt if they are lacking in income. But I think I should work to earn my keep."

"I don't know what kind of work a young woman might do in Saint Charles."

"Oh, I could become a seamstress or housemaid. You know my formal schooling ended when I was thirteen."

Blue Feather nodded and was silent for a few minutes. But Louise Marie wanted to continue the conversation, which she thought was good for them both. "What do you think you will do? Will you go back to your farm?"

"I haven't decided yet. I could farm again or perhaps I could sign on as a scout for a wagon train. Some months ago, there was fair amount of wagon trains starting out of either Saint Louis or Saint Charles."

"Blue Feather you have that college education you could put to good use, don't you? Perhaps you could find work as a teacher or in an office downtown."

"Well, that didn't work out a few years ago when I had just graduated. Some potential employers were shocked to see an Indian when I appeared for an interview. I was up against some serious prejudices, I suppose."

"I'm sorry to hear that! When we met, I suspected you had some Indian blood. But you were wearing an Army uniform – there can't be many full-blooded Indians in uniform."

"No, there aren't any that I know of. But I guess I'm just caught between two cultures."

One morning a few days later into their trip, Louise Marie took ill. "I think that the water we drank from that last stream has made me a bit sick."

"Well, I only drank the chicory we made after it was steaming hot. I'm not feeling poorly at all. But you should lie down on your bed roll in the wagon until you feel better."

The next day they entered Saint Charles and Louise Marie was able to find their way to her relatives' home. There was a vacant lot nearby where they parked their covered wagon. Louise Marie walked up the wooden stairs to the porch and knocked on the door. A black woman answered the door and was startled when she saw the girl standing there. "Oh, it cain't be! Ain't you Miss Louise Blanchette?"

"Yes, and you are Annabelle, are you not? Are my aunt and uncle home?"

"Ah thought ah was seein a ghost, honey child! No, your relatives moved back east when they got word that you all were killt by dem Injuns! We thought you were all daid!"

"I was the only survivor, and I was taken captive by the Comanches. Then the Caddo Indians rescued me, and I lived with them for four years. They are a civilized tribe and treated me well. Do you know what city my relatives moved to?"

"Dey talked about Evansville or Cincinnati. But I never got the final word. Dey sold me to the new massuh who bought this here house because I aksed dem to. Ah has fambly here. Dese new massuhs be nice folks, a preacher man and his wife and chilluns."

"I'm not sure what to do, Miss Annabelle. I don't have the means to go searching for them."

"Maybe da pastors at Saint Charles Borromeo have an address for dem. Maybe you stop by there for help."

"That's good advice, thank you Miss Annabelle. I'll do that."

"Child, ah is just so happy to see you alive! Say now, dat hansum man walkin dis way, he be your husband?

"Yes, he is. We are newlyweds," thinking that this would preclude any suspicion of sinfulness.

"Oh, dat be music to mah ears!"

When Blue Feather walked up, Louise Marie told him what happened. Blue Feather said, "Let's do stop by Saint Charles Borromeo to see if your relatives left a forwarding address. Then I think you should come with me to my farm, and we can figure what to do next and not be in any rush."

At Saint Charles Borromeo the secretary told them that the church did not keep such records, but suggested they go to St. Peter's to check with Fr. Koenig, who had been a friend of theirs who had since be assigned to a new parish.

At St. Peter's they were greeted warmly by Fr. Koenig, who had been friendly with the Blanchette family. Unfortunately, Fr. Koenig did not have any information on Louise Marie's relatives except that they had settled in Cincinnati. "Perhaps I can still help you. I can write to the bishop in Cincinnati and explain the situation. He can poll the pastors in his diocese to see where the Blanchettes now go to church. Will you be staying in this area for some time? This process could take weeks or months."

"Yes, Father. We'll be staying at my farm which is nearby. Louise Marie and I are newlyweds."

Louise Marie smiled when Blue Feather described them as newlyweds. *Perhaps all this meant was that he was trying to protect my reputation, but I hope that it means more,* she thought.

When they were seated on the covered wagon again, Blue Feather turned to her and said, "We can live at my farm until you decide what to do about contacting your relatives."

"Will you be staying with me?"

Blue Feather paused for a few seconds before he replied, "I will, at least until I figure out what I need to do. I mean, I could join a wagon train as their scout, or I could try to find work in Saint Louis, or I could stay at the farm. I just don't know."

"Why would you want to leave your farm and ... me behind?"

"Louise Marie, I just need some time to mourn Winnie on my own, and to think through what this means in my life."

"OK, I think I understand. But you will come back to me, won't you?"

"Yes, I'll come back. I just don't know when."

♋   ♋   ♋

It was late afternoon when Blue Feather and Louise Marie pulled up to the Chouteau farmhouse. Blue Feather helped Louise Marie down from the wagon and led her to the door which was unlocked. She walked in and took a quick look around the place she thought would serve as her temporary home. Blue Feather brought their rather sparse belongings in from the wagon and then unharnessed the mules and led them to stalls in the barn, then he led his fine chestnut horse to its stall and put on the animals' feedbags.

Shamus, White Fawn, and their children must have seen the covered wagon pull in and they quickly traversed the fifty yards or so that separated their homes. Shamus called out,

"Blue Feather, it's so good to see you! We knew your enlistment was over, but we were unsure of your next steps."

"To be honest, I'm not sure of anything, either."

At that moment Louise Marie stepped out of the house and walked up to the others standing there.

"Hello, I am Louise Marie Blanchette. You must be Shamus and White Fawn – Blue Feather has told me about your wonderful friendship."

White Fawn spoke up first, "We are pleased to meet you, Louise Marie. How did you meet Blue Feather?"

Blue Feather jumped in and answered for her, "Louise Marie and I met at a Caddo Indian village in northeast Texas. She had been living with the Caddo tribe since she was 13. The Caddo tribe rescued her from the Comanches who had killed everyone else in her parents' wagon train which had just arrived in Texas from Saint Charles."

White Fawn sighed and said, "I am so sorry to hear of your loss! Did you want to return to Saint Charles because you have family there?"

"Yes, I thought there was a good chance that my aunt and uncle were still living here; but we found that they had moved to Cincinnati. Father Koenig at St. Peters is trying to locate them for me."

"In the meantime, Louise Marie will be staying at the farm here," said Blue Feather.

"Well, tonight we want you to join us for dinner at our place. You must be tired from all your travel."

"Thank you, White Fawn. I'll come with you now to help you prepare the meal."

As the women left to prepare the meal, Shamus spoke to Blue Feather about the recent harvest of corn, the harvest of vegetables, and the condition of his livestock. Shamus had taken care of everything quite well, and Blue Feather was quite pleased.

"After dinner, the two couples were discussing recent events in Louise Marie's life. White Fawn asked, "When you reconnect with your relatives and go to Ohio to live with them, will you go to school or find a job?" Then with a wink, "Or will you find a husband?"

Then somewhat timidly, Louis Marie responded, "Actually, I already have a husband. Blue Feather married me so that I could leave the Caddo village with him. This is the only way a Caddo girl can leave her village. She can get married and go to the village of her husband."

Blue Feather could read the surprise and perhaps indignation on his friends' faces and said, "This wedding began as a deception so that Louise Marie could return to live with her people. But, then..."

"We consummated the marriage that night! I'm embarrassed and sorry to say that I tempted Blue Feather beyond his control."

"You must not assume all the blame – I acted on my physical desire and was unfaithful to Winnie."

"When were your married?" asked Shamus.

"It was four weeks ago."

"Blue Feather, your dear Winnie passed away five weeks ago. Technically, you were eligible to marry Louise Marie."

"That might be the case, but I didn't yet know of her death. I did not pick up your letter until a day later when we stopped at Fort Smith."

"So, in your mind you were sinning by being unfaithful to Winnie."

White Fawn, wanting to alleviate some of their guilt said, "Oh, but many Indian tribes allow a man to have multiple wives. It was not really a sin for you to marry..."

This drew a sharp look from Blue Feather and White Fawn quit talking.

After a few seconds of embarrassed silence Blue Feather and White Fawn rose to thank their hosts and return to Blue Feather's farmhouse.

That night they shared the large bed and Blue Feather tenderly knew Louise Marie for the first time since their wedding night.

When Louise Marie got up the next morning, she looked around the house briefly hoping to see Blue Feather. Instead, she found a note:

Dear Louise Marie,

THE EARLY YEARS OF BLUE FEATHER • 143

I need some time alone and away from familiar places that call to mind my late wife. This farm, house, my friends – they all remind me of Winnie. Wagon trains are leaving Westport Missouri all the time, so I'm going to ride my chestnut up the Missouri to see if a wagon train needs a scout or wagon train captain. I don't know how long I will be away. I must work through my grief, and then I will return to you.

You should realize now that I love you, but I don't feel that I deserve you right now. I still feel guilt over my infidelity – I have confessed it, and I know that I have been forgiven, but I don't feel like I deserve happiness just yet.

Shamus and White Fawn will watch over you. Part of what Shamus earns through the sale of my crops or livestock is rightfully yours. Shamus will not need to be reminded of that. Also, I have left some cash from my Army pay in the cash box I showed you last night. That money is for you to spend as you see fit.

I'm sorry to surprise you with this unannounced departure but I thought if I waited any longer, I would never go.

Much love to you,

Your husband, Blue Feather

Louise Marie was sitting on the steps to her porch when White Fawn arrived with a basket of eggs. She was holding the letter and crying.

"Oh, honey whatever is wrong?"

Louis Marie simply held up the letter to White Fawn, who said, "I'm sorry, but I can't read. I was brought up as an Indian without any schooling, you know. You'll have to tell me what it says."

White Fawn sat down next to Louise Marie as she read the letter aloud. When she finished reading White Fawn hugged her and said, "Don't worry a bit, Louise Marie. Blue Feather said he loves you and that he'll return. He needs to work through his grief and his guilt, and when he does that, he'll be back. I know Blue Feather – he is loyal and true to his word. But I've got to admit, I am mad at him for sneaking out like this! Oh, that Blue Feather! He'd rather face an angry bear or mountain lion than a woman who was bound to be disappointed with him!"

Louise Marie got an anxious look on her face, and then quickly stood up and ran a couple of steps. Then she vomited. "Oh, excuse me! I think I drank some tainted water on our journey."

"But that was a few days ago. It couldn't still be... Louise Marie, are you late getting your period?"

"Yes, but... Oh no, you don't think this means I'm with child?"

"Yes, I do believe that is what is happening here. You're going to have a baby!"

CHAPTER TWELVE

Blue Feather followed the Missouri River west until he reached Independence, Missouri. At this location, wagon trains were forming, most of which were headed up the Oregon Trail. As Blue Feather rode through the staging area where a variety of wagon trains were forming, he came across an old friend. A rugged looking man dressed like a frontiersman looked up as Blue Feather rode by.

"Well, if it isn't Blue Feather the Osage scout! It has been years! What brings you to this staging area?"

"Captain Jedidiah Gregg! It's good to see you! Are you leading a wagon train to the Northwest?"

"Yes, I am! Would you be looking for a job as a scout? Because if your answer is yes, you are hired!"

"I'd be pleased to work with you again, Captain!"

"Excellent! I see that you have your bedroll, canteen, mess kit, and weapons with you. Do you need a pup tent?"

"Ve have vun you can use, Herr Blue Feather!"

Blue Feather looked over to source of the voice, and it was Gertrude and Heinrich De Jong, the cooks, and their adopted son Johannes.

"Wow! I am really happy to see you! So, you signed on for this trek as well?"

"Ja, ve go mit Herr Hauptmann Gregg everywhere!"

"And this young man must be Johannes – you are growing up!"

"Yes, and believe me, I am grateful that I am growing up with the De Jongs and not with the Comanches."

"Captain Gregg, when do you plan to depart, and what is your destination?"

"At first light tomorrow morning we will be setting off for Oregon Territory."

"I'll be ready! But first I must write my friends a letter to let them know where I'll be. I expect that it would be about eight months for a round trip."

"That's a hopeful guess, could be a month longer depending on conditions."

Louise Marie was surprised to get a letter from Blue Feather. Postmarked a week earlier in Independence Missouri, it said that he loved her and would return in eight months. He reconnected with some old friends, a Captain Gregg, who was leading a wagon train of thirty families, and the De Jong family, including their adopted son, Johannes. Blue Feather would be traveling with them as their scout.

"Well, at least he said he loves me, and it sounds like he will have good friends to keep him company. But eight months is a long time! I probably will have my baby by then," Louise Marie said to herself, her eyes moistening with tears.

Just then White Fawn walked in and said, "I could not help but hear what you said. Don't worry – Blue Feather's word is as good as gold."

The morning of their departure Blue Feather walked with Captain Gregg as he went up and down the line of wagons joining his train. Johannes tagged along out of curiosity.

"Johannes, you can see that we have at least two kinds of wagons joining us. There are some big Conestoga wagons pulled by a team of four or six mules or oxen. The front and back of the wagon were built higher than the middle, and there is a high, rounded, white canvas roof. Some folks call them camels of the prairie. This smaller and less sturdy model is called a prairie schooner."

"Will we have to cross rivers? We are going to have herds of cows and horses with us, aren't we? How will we get them across the deeper rivers?"

Blue Feather answered Johannes, "To float the wagons across, I will show the men how to make dugout canoes that can be lashed together, or better, connected by planks. The wheels of the wagons will roll into the dugout canoes. For the herds, we'll have to build larger rafts. We will pole our way across, or we can set up a tow line. A Missourian by the name of David Hickman designed a type of pulley system that works well."

"Say, look at this fancy carriage! Are they going with us?" asked Johannes.

A bit of a grimace showed on Captain Gregg's face, "As a matter of fact, they are. There's an English fellow, Thomas Clark, who is moving his family west to Oregon. This includes his mother, a 25-year-old sister named Grace, a 17-year-old brother named Hodgson, another brother named Charlie, and a married sister with husband and two children. I got to know this family fairly well because Thomas had made this trip with me before, in 1848. He is a good man, rugged enough for the west, but I'm not sure about the rest of the family. He had this rig custom-built so that his sister could drive their mother in comfort and style. This cushioned rocking chair is bolted to the floor of the carriage. It's more rugged than the usual street carriage, but as far as I know, it is the first of its kind to make this journey."

"I guess there's a first time for everything! I just hope Clark's family members toughen up quickly, and I hope they brought some spare parts for this fancy rig."

Their conversation was interrupted by a rider followed by a pack of five hunting hounds each trying to out-bark the other. Seeing Captain Gregg, he pulled up and dismounted.

"Good day gentlemen! I apologize for the bloody racket these hounds are making. We are just now returning from a run in the country. The hounds need their exercise, you know!"

Blue Feather asked, "Did you do a lot of hunting in England?"

"Oh, I would go on the fox hunt with my hounds, on occasion. But there isn't much big game left in England. Of course, I did do a fair amount of target practice to maintain the skills I learned at Sandhurst."

Noting the blank look on his audience's faces he said, "Sandhurst is the Royal Military Academy, where all fine English chaps earn their commissions."

"So, you have some military experience?" Asked Blue Feather.

"Why yes, of course! I was in India for the war with the Sikhs in 1845 and 1846. Why do you ask, sir?"

"Because we might need every man we can muster to ward off hostile Indian attacks."

Clark looked at Captain Gregg, "Why should there be any trouble? We didn't run into any hostiles on our trip in 1848."

"The situation has changed. Some tribes are getting anxious about all the white settlers taking over their hunting grounds and scaring off the buffalo. Last year, 50,000 white settlers traveled to the northwest and this year there will be more!" said Captain Gregg.

"Then perhaps I should hire a man to guard my family at all times," Clark said, glancing at Blue Feather.

But before Blue Feather could say anything, Captain Gregg spoke up, "My friend here, Blue Feather Chouteau, has been hired as our scout for this journey. He can't do both jobs."

"Oh, jolly well then! I'm sure I can find someone in this large company of pioneers."

"Let me suggest that you make friends with another family where the man looks like he can handle himself in a skirmish and have your families travel together."

"I say, that is a splendid idea, old chap!"

The trek to Oregon Territory was peaceful at first, with the settlers actually doing some trading with Indian tribes along the way through the rolling hills of northeastern Kansas. Crossing into Nebraska, the route followed the South Platte River for a distance, with the wagon train making camp along one of the many freshwater streams that fed into the Platte River. The river itself was not inviting. The river was "too thin to plow and too thick to drink." Travelers would fill their pots and kettles and let the vessels sit for a few hours for the silt to settle. Then they would boil up their cornmeal.

But these popular camping grounds had become contaminated after several thousands of travelers had passed through the route. There were no sewage facilities or treatment plants – these would not become available until decades in the future. The result was cholera with the acute symptom of diarrhea, which only added to the contamination.

When people started getting sick, Blue Feather took action. He reasoned that a wagon train was essentially a moving town, one that, in fact, required families to live in close proximity to each other. This was like the situation in Saint Louis which had been ravaged by cholera, losing about ten percent of its population. In that city people were living in crowded conditions and there was no sewer system. Blue Feather reasoned that families needed to spread out more and not dump their waste into the river or stream but bury it. He also reasoned that if contamination was in the water, it might be purified by boiling it.

When the first four cases of cholera broke out in quick succession, Blue Feather told Captain Gregg his idea and a wagon train meeting was called. Blue Feather explained to everyone what they needed to do. Some travelers were skeptical but agreed to comply with the advice anyway. The plan was implemented too late for some people. The original four cases ended in death and another six followed, totaling 10 deaths out of 30 persons infected in a population of 119. After a nervous wait of two days no new cases became apparent, and the people broke camp and resumed the journey.

Some days later the wagon train stopped at Fort Kearny to replenish their provisions.

"Not much of a fort from the looks of things – there's no palisade or watch towers," said Johannes, who was riding with Blue Feather.

"You are right in saying this isn't much of a fort. Fortunately, the Indians in these parts, the Omaha Sioux, have been friendly and not bothered by all the white settlers traveling through their land. Besides, the white settlers bring goods for trade that the Omaha desire. But you know, that could all change."

"You mean that the Omaha could get fed up with the white settlers? I imagine that the situation would get worse if white settlers decided to settle in these parts rather than going the full course to Oregon."

"That is a possibility. Another possibility is that one tribe could wage war on a second tribe, like the Pawnees against the Omaha. When resources like prime hunting grounds and clean water become scarce competition for them can become fierce."

"Why would that matter to most white people if the Indians want to kill each other?"

Blue Feather sighed and looked at Johannes until he had eye contact, "Johannes, if any group of persons is suffering, white, black, Indian, Mexican – it doesn't matter what groups are involved – as Christians we should care. We are all God's children, it's just that some of us don't realize it yet."

"OK, I guess that I will always be angry with the Comanches for what they did to my parents, especially my mother. I don't think I'll ever get over that."

"Well, I understand. It seems that some sins, the most heinous of sins like what happened to your parents, are unforgivable. But Father De Smet taught me that if I could forgive others for their transgressions, then God the Father will also forgive me. But if I could not forgive others, then the Father will not forgive my sins."

"Blue Feather do you really believe in all that Bible stuff?"

Blue Feather was silent for a few seconds before he answered, "Yes, but I admit that at times my faith is challenged. Honestly, I don't think I could have any peace in my heart if I didn't have the little faith that I do have. I pray to God to help my unbelief."

A day later it became time to ford the North Platte River at the mouth of Deer Creek. It was running fast and deep after days of rain to the northwest. Captain Gregg called another wagon meeting to tell the travelers of his plan.

"Folks, this here river is running pretty fast and it's deeper than nine feet at the center. Now that's too deep for our livestock to swim and there is no way that your teams could pull your wagons across. Blue Feather, here, is going to show us how we can build rafts to haul our wagons across and larger rafts to haul the livestock across. I have led many a wagon train this way and they all have crossed this river. You all can do this, I know it!"

Blue Feather started his instruction, "Before we begin, we'll need to collect our tools. Ideally, we would find axes, some broad adzes, curved knives, wedges, D-adzes, elbow adzes, and some cooper's adzes. Raise your hand if you have some of these tools."

Several men raised their hands and Blue Feather asked them to bring their tools to the construction staging area.

"Now, I should have asked this question earlier – are there any fellows here who have some skills or experience that would be especially useful in this project?"

A few men raised their hands. One said he was carpenter and a sawyer, another a woodworker, a third a cooper, and a fourth a boatwright. The young man who was a boatwright also volunteered, "Not only am I a boatwright, I also built some dugout canoes with my grandfather, who is a Powhattan Indian."

Blue Feather was elated to hear this, "Great, then each of us can lead a construction crew!"

"Our first step is to find two straight trees that will give us a log at least twelve feet long at the widest part of the tree. Indians preferred pine and chestnut, but spruce, cottonwood, and cedar can also serve the purpose."

The work was well underway when two boys ran up with exciting news, "We found a bunch of canoes underwater upstream from here! They were in shallow water with lots of rocks weighing them down!"

Blue Feather was surprised to hear this news, then after a couple of seconds he responded,

"Well, that is good news indeed. Because that means someone made these canoes and left them here for others to use."

"But storing them underwater? Wouldn't it make more sense to flip them upside down and store them on dry ground?" asked Nathan the boatwright.

"One might think so, but I have heard of the practice among some Indian tribes. In a cold climate like this, freezing rain and heavy snow can cause the canoes to crack. Stored in the water deep enough not to freeze, the canoes fare much better."

Blue Feather and some other men jogged over to the submerged canoes and pulled them out of the water and turned them over. Then they inspected them for cracks and to see if the wood was water-logged. It turned out that the canoes were in good condition, the only effect of being submerged was that some of the bark was coming loose – but that was not a problem. Between the two canoes they were building and the eight recovered canoes they had four to build two rafts for transporting two wagons at a time and still have six canoes to use in building two livestock rafts. Blue Feather asked the carpenter and boatwright to the lead the construction of the raft.

They would need sturdy poles possibly 12 feet long to pole the canoes across the river. So Blue Foot described what was needed to the gang of ten boys hanging out by the construction site and set them loose with some axes in search of young trees that met the criteria. The boys did not fail him – they returned with 12 poles of the appropriate length. For their part, Sam the carpenter/sawyer and Nathan the boatwright cut some planks to connect the canoes and built the raft.

A few of the travelers grew impatient with all the construction and decided to try another means of crossing the river. They applied tar to the seams of their prairie schooners to make them watertight and disassembled the running gear and stored it on the wagon. The team of four fine Missouri mules was released from their harnesses and led into the water by a drover and made to swim across. In the wagon-turned-boat a man stood up to pole his way across the river. It turned out that this method was no faster than the raft method led by Blue Feather, counting the time disassembling the running gear, caulking the seams on the body of the wagon, and then reassembling the wagon on the other side.

A young couple from Sweden who tried the same manner of crossing the river, met with tragedy. Inger Thoresen fell overboard and was carried away from the converted wagon by the swift current. Her husband, Erik, riding the lead mule through the river didn't notice right away. By the time he noticed, she was 50 yards downstream and going under. Erik wasn't a skilled swimmer, but he jumped in trying to rescue her. Both of them ended up drowning.

That evening Blue Feather was invited to share a late meal with the De Jongs. As they sat around the campfire, they spoke of the day's events. Then after a pause in the conversation, Gertrude said quietly, almost to herself, "Vell, at least Inger and Erik died together and now are in himel mit our Lord."

Blue Feather responded quietly in the same manner, "Yes, if only it had been that way for Winnie and me."

$$\text{\textcloseleaf} \quad \text{\textcloseleaf} \quad \text{\textcloseleaf}$$

The trek was uneventful with the exception of a broken axle on one wagon and a broken wheel on another. When one traveler broke down, all wagons stopped and the men with the most skills helped fix or replace the broken part.

Mrs. Clark's fancy carriage was holding up well, with no break-downs yet. Had there been a problem, help was never but a few feet away. At any point in time there were at least three young single men walking alongside the carriage, vying for the attention of Miss Clark, who was a stunning young blonde of 25 years. The would-be suitors were testing their courage and resolve because prim and proper Mrs. Clark's glare at these unworthy suitors (and they were all unworthy) could ward off a mountain lion.

CHAPTER THIRTEEN

T
he wagon train was about three miles south of Fort Laramie in Wyoming Territory when they came upon a large Indian settlement. There were teepees of various tribes there, including the Lakota Sioux, Cheyenne, Assiniboine, Gros Ventre, Mandan, Arikara, Hidatsa, Shoshone, Crow, and Arapaho, and Blue Feather marveled at the sight, because he could identify them by the markings on their teepees. *But what would bring the chiefs from such disparate nations together?* wondered Blue Feather. And then he saw the U.S. Army officers and he concluded that leaders from each tribe were taking part in treaty discussions with the U.S. government.

As they drew nearer Blue Feather saw a figure in black speaking with some chiefs, and his heart skipped a beat. *Could it be? What a coincidence it would be if that black robe was none other than Father De Smet!*

Blue Feather directed his horse into the temporary village housing the visiting chiefs and their entourages, heading toward the priest.

Father De Smet identified Blue Feather right away, even before Blue Feather pulled up and dismounted.

"Blue Feather! What a sight for sore eyes! How are you? What brings you to Fort Laramie? I am here helping the federal government negotiate a peace treaty among various tribes and safe passage for the white emigrants on the Oregon Trail. We have reached a roadblock because I can't make myself understood to the Cheyenne and Blackfoot chiefs. Can you visit for say, an hour, this evening to meet with me and Chief Black Wolf in this teepee here?"

"Yes, the wagon train I am scouting for will be spending the night a few minutes from here. But seeing you Father, I am reminded that I need you to hear my confession!"

"We can do that now, if you are available. My teepee is the one with the cross on the entrance flap."

When they were alone in Fr. De Smet's teepee, Blue Feather told Father De Smet the whole story of the past months. Including of course, his sin of adultery with Louise Marie.

"Father, I admit I sinned with Louise Marie. I let my physical attraction cloud my judgment and we consummated our fake marriage. At that point I didn't know that Winnie had died of the cholera in Saint Louis a week before the wedding with Louise Marie. Did God punish me by taking Winnie before I actually sinned?"

"No," Father De Smet said firmly, "Although God knew what you were going to do, before you even thought of doing it, He would not punish you in advance of your sin. Tell me, Blue Feather, do you love this girl that you took as your wife in the Caddo village?"

"Yes, I think I do. But I am sure that I loved Winnie more."

"That is understandable – your love will grow in time if you act out of love. Do you intend to keep Louise Marie as your wife? Even though you were not married within the Catholic church, you promised to love and care for this young woman."

"I will honor my promise to her, and we will get married again in the Catholic church."

"It pleases me to hear that! But now I must strongly advise you to return to Missouri as soon as possible. You should not have left her the way you did. Now, before you do anything else, sit down here at my field desk and write Louise Marie a letter. Apologize for leaving her alone so abruptly and tell her when you will return."

"You are being rather bossy and impatient with me, Father," said Blue Feather looking a little miffed.

"From what I've heard, it seems that you need some forceful direction right now. And I will not hide my disappointment in you – you knew better, and you are a better man than this."

Blue Feather feeling properly chastised looked down at his boots. "I will do everything you say, and do whatever penance you require, but will this remove the guilt and shame I feel?"

"You are feeling estranged from God right now. The only thing you can do is pray and reflect on God's word and listen for the Lord. Here, take my Bible and turn to Jeremiah chapter 29 and read aloud starting with verse 11 until I ask you to stop."

Blue Feather took the Bible and read aloud, "For I know the thoughts that I think toward you, says the Lord, thoughts of peace and not of evil, to give you a future and a hope. Then you will call upon Me and go and pray to Me, and I will listen to you. And you will seek Me and find Me, when you search for Me with all your heart. I will be found by you, says the Lord, and I will bring you back from your captivity; I will gather you from all the nations and from all the places where I have driven you, says the Lord, and I will bring you to the place from which I caused you to be carried away captive."

"OK, stop there. Now let's discuss this."

"Father, I don't quite understand how this passage applies to my situation."

Father De Smet thought for a couple of seconds before he responded, "The Jews were being held in captivity in Babylon, a foreign land. They had been unfaithful and disobedient to God, and God allowed the Babylonians to destroy Jerusalem, and march the inhabitants off to captivity in Babylon. Because of your sin, young man, you are feeling estranged from God and feeling chastised by Him. But know this – God still loves you and has only good things in mind for you. However, you must humble yourself and approach God in prayer, seeking Him with all your heart.

Then He will hear you and release you from this captivity of guilt and shame. This will not happen overnight, but if you earnestly seek Him, He will come to you."

"Blue Feather, relief will eventually come."

Blue Feather sat silently for a few seconds and then sighed.

"I realize now that I have sinned against Louise Marie, and I will return to her as soon as possible."

"Blue Feather, write to Louise Marie now and tell her that you will be returning to her upon completing your contract with Captain Gregg. You should be home in four months, perhaps? I will mail the letter from the first post office on the Missouri River that I encounter. It should be just weeks before it finds its way to St. Peters, Missouri.

මෙ   මෙ   මෙ

The next day Blue Feather shared breakfast with Fr. De Smet and upon finishing, they walked and prayed together. As they were concluding their prayers young Johannes rode up hoping to fetch Blue Feather. Father De Smet looked up at the boy on his Appaloosa mare and the boy looked down at Fr. De Smet and they simultaneously exclaimed, "My rescuer!" Then they both laughed. Johannes dismounted quickly and the priest and the boy hugged in the manner of men.

"It's so good to see you, Johannes! You have grown so much – you are a young man now!"

"And I have you to thank that I was able to grow up with a Christian family instead of those God-less Comanches!"

"Johannes, I think that we must thank God for delivering us. Without him both of us would be lost!"

"Fr. De Smet, it is time for Johannes and me to leave. For now, we must say goodbye. But you have my address in St. Charles County, Missouri. Please write me when you have some time for a visit in Saint Louis."

"I will indeed, my son!"

♋   ♋   ♋

CHAPTER FOURTEEN

Cho Cho Co (Has No Horse) and his raiding party hid in a copse of trees near the Raft River where it joins the Snake River in Idaho Territory. Barely 20 years of age, he was already an experienced warrior and leader of this particular band of Shoshone. Cho Cho Co said in a low voice to those who were close by, "Look at these foolish women. They did the same thing yesterday. They drove their fancy carriage way ahead of the rest of the wagon train to stop and rest and eat a meal. They have no men to protect them, just a boy who hasn't yet seen 17 summers, and I don't see any weapons on them."

"Let us attack now!" urged a rather impetuous brave still in his teens.

"No, let us wait and see if more riders arrive to water their horses at the river. We are here to steal their horses."

An ugly overweight brave said, "Well, I want that young blonde woman. She is worth three horses to me. She would make a good wife."

"Well, her figure is appealing, and it would be pleasurable to know her, but she is fragile, even for a white woman. She is probably not used to the work a Shoshone woman must do. But you may have her if you still desire her once you see her close up."

"If I don't want her, I will take her scalp!"

Shortly afterwards, a small herd of horses arrived followed by some beef cattle. They were being driven by four mounted cowboys.

"Ah, just what we have been waiting for! We outnumber the white men three to one. This should not be any trouble."

"Wait! I want twelve braves to attack the wagon train. Your main goal is to capture as many horses as you can from the whites. If you see a woman or girl you want, you may take her too. But first you must capture the horses."

"Let's attack the whites now with full fury!"

With that, the raiding party numbering about 24 braves mounted their horses and galloped toward the party preparing their lunch and the cowboys behind them watching over the horses as they watered.

The raiders charged at the startled Mrs. Clark and her 25-year-old daughter, Grace. The drovers thinking only of themselves, quickly took refuge behind some big rocks next to the river. A warrior, much older than the others in the raiding party, started to unhitch some horses from a wagon driven by one of the drovers. Hodgson ran to the carriage to retrieve a pistol he brought but as he climbed into the carriage he was pierced by an arrow. Mrs. Clark screamed at the man stealing the horses, but the man turned and aimed his rifle at her. Grace scrambled on top of her mother to protect her, but a bullet shot clean through her wrist and into her mother's heart.

The warriors then turned to Grace, a tall brave grabbing her and throwing her to the ground. An ugly fat warrior said, "Bah, she is too skinny – you can have her."

Then the tall warrior tore off her clothes intending to violate her. She resisted strenuously and was shot in the upper chest. Perhaps again because of her thin frame, the bullet exited her body through the armpit. Then she played dead. Disgusted with this turn of events, the Shoshones threw her down the bluff overlooking the river and rolled stones on her.

In the meantime, Thomas Clark had heard the gunfire and had hastily returned from duck hunting followed by his baying hounds. Thomas's gallop along with his eight hounds kicked up a lot of dust, and the Shoshones thought that this could only be a large group of riders coming to the rescue. The drovers behind the rocks opened fire on the Indians who returned fire.

Back with the main body of the wagon train, Blue Feather had been riding with Johannes at his side intending to check in on the Clark family. Not finding their carriage in the usual place in the train, Blue Feather swore to himself and said to Johannes, "I am afraid that the Clark women and young Hodgson had followed Thomas Clark when he went ahead to go duck hunting. If so, that was a bad idea to leave the protection of the wagon train. They did this before, and I warned them about it."

Then they heard the gunfire ahead and Blue Feather turned to Johannes and said, "This could be an Indian raid. You should return to your parents and help them defend themselves!"

When the boy hesitated, Blue Feather forcefully said, "Go now!!!" Then he spurred his horse to gallop to the site where he thought the Clark family would be. But by this point in time, the raiders who had been sent to attack the main body of the wagon train were speeding toward him. Blue Feather found a large boulder and quickly dismounted and began firing at the raiders as they galloped toward him. His bullets hit one horse which collapsed and rolled over on its rider. The raiders were not really interested in engaging him in battle because the prize, the settlers' herd of horses, was their target. As they sped by, Blue Feather realized they weren't going to fight him and quickly mounted and pursued them in full gallop. He didn't start shooting again until he pulled alongside the raiders. His fire killed or wounded another raider who fell from his horse.

Captain Gregg, alerted by Johannes, realized that an attack was imminent, and he had the wagons drawn into a circle. The last gap was about to close when Blue Feather galloped through. He immediately joined Captain Gregg in getting the settlers situated to return fire.

As the Shoshone raiders galloped around the circle of wagons shooting at the settlers, the settlers, mostly farmers, returned fire. But these men were not yet hardened to the west and except for a few veterans of the Mexican war, had not fired weapons at human beings before. Only a few Indians and their horses were hit.

Thomas Clark remained at the site of the first attack. Some of the drovers helped him pick up the bodies of his mother and younger brother and put them in the wagon bed. Finding Grace was next. He and the drovers figured her for dead from the gunshot to the chest and if not that alone, being tossed down a bluff and being covered by stones, should have taken her life.

A drover pointed to the bluff where he had seen Grace being thrown down. He went with Clark to help him uncover her and carry her back to the carriage for transport to the wagon train.

They picked the stones off her presumed corpse but were startled to see Grace breathing! She wasn't conscious, but she was alive. Thomas picked up his sister and carried her to the carriage where he gently set her down. Then he retrieved his horse and tied her reins to the carriage.

Back at the wagon train Blue Feather had switched to his bow and arrow as his ammunition ran out. With the bow he was able to drop two more Shoshone. Then the Shoshone decided to quit their attack. They had lost five of their warriors and had noticed there weren't any additional horses to steal. They picked up their dead and wounded and fled to their campsite.

Arriving at the circle of wagons, Thomas Clark yelled for someone to get the doctor. Fortunately, it was too early in the day for the good physician to be completely soused, so he was competent to take care of Grace. Thomas Clark was sure she would die, especially if moved and he persuaded Captain Gregg to remain encamped for at least three days. Captain Gregg said, "Well, let's hear what the doctor has to say."

Thomas and Captain Gregg consulted with the physician after he had tended to her. The physician, Dr. Andrew Belmont of Missouri, told them, "Grace's condition is serious, but she could recover. She has two wounds where the bullets had passed through her thin body, one in the wrist and the second in the chest with an exit wound in the armpit. She also has a fractured leg from being rolled down a steep bluff, scratches, and abrasions from the tumble down the bluff, and wounds on her head where she was struck by stones her abusers had rolled down on her. I want to keep her in bed and not move her for two days at least."

Charles Clark wanted to avenge the death of his mother and his younger brother, and the young single men of the company who were very fond of Grace wanted revenge. There were three horses not attached to wagons. These were saddled and Charles Clark and two of Grace's would-be suitors were about to take off for the wagon train led by Americus Savage which they knew was few hours ahead of their own. At this wagon train they hoped to recruit fifteen armed men on good horses to track down the Shoshones, get revenge, and reclaim the lost horses. Blue Feather felt like his duty was to stay with the wagons and Captain Gregg agreed – they didn't know if the Shoshone would return and re-sume their attack.

Blue Feather warned the young men before they took off,

"You're likely to be greatly outnumbered by the Shoshone, and they might be waiting to ambush you if a scout notices you coming. Don't forget, this is their home territory, and they know it like the backs of their hands."

"We're not fools, Blue Feather! If we can catch up with the Americus Savage train, we'll recruit at least a dozen men to run down these Injuns and make them pay for what they did to Grace and her family, and we'll get those horses back."

"Even a hundred men might not be enough! This is their home, and their village could have several hundred men. I would not risk my life for revenge or for a few horses."

The three young men waved off Blue Feather dismissively and galloped off in search of the wagon train ahead of them. Once they found the other wagon train, they were able to recruit twelve men to join their quest, selling them on the idea that it would be good to end the Shoshone threat once and for all.

The posse of fifteen men rode hard in pursuit of the Shoshone and reached their location by early afternoon. They saw the stolen horses grazing peacefully on a hillside seemingly unattended.

The posse continued riding to the hill and then galloped up the hill to round up the stolen herd of horses. Suddenly the Shoshone sprang up from behind boulders and large bushes and fired their guns and arrows into the unsuspecting posse. One horse and its rider were killed and one of the volunteers was wounded. Charles quickly realized that the Indians had a natural fortress that could not be breached and decided their mission was doomed for failure. There would be no revenge for the deaths in his family, and no stolen horses would be recovered. As the posse made their hasty retreat, Charles's mind went back to Blue Feather's warning which they had chosen to ignore. He resolved to listen next time.

ℭ ℭ ℭ

Blue Feather and Captain Gregg were visiting Grace Clark as she convalesced in her makeshift bed.

"It is so nice of you to stop by and see me, gentlemen! I'm afraid I won't be much company in my sad and sorry state – what hurts more than my injuries is the loss of my mother and younger brother. I might not ever recover from that horrible attack."

"We understand, Miss Clark. We just wanted to check in with you and express our condolences," said Captain Gregg.

"And I just wanted to tell you that I will be praying for your comfort as you mourn your mother and brother. I recently lost my wife to the cholera epidemic, and I too am grieving," said Blue Feather.

"I am so sorry for your loss, Mr. Chouteau!"

Captain Gregg heard his name being called, and he excused himself.

"I assume that there will be no way the murderers can be brought to justice."

"No, the Shoshone tribe is nomadic, and the raiders are probably long gone by now."

"But what about the white men posing as Indians – they would not be traveling with the Shoshone, would they?

Blue Feather was shocked. "There were white men in that raiding party?"

"Yes! There were at least two, and one of them had blue eyes and a sandy beard."

"Can you describe them for me, give me more details about their appearance?"

"Well, the one with the blue eyes and sandy beard was quite tall, I'd say 6 foot 3 inches, slender, but strong."

"How do you know he was strong?"

"Because he was the one who pulled me out of the carriage and threw me to the ground like I was nothing more than a rag doll!"

"Young, middle-aged, or old?"

"Definitely young – I'd guess mid-twenties."

"Anything else about this particular man that you can recall?"

"Oh, yes! He appeared to be wearing some kind of white undergarment beneath his buckskin Indian outfit."

"Really? I wonder...perhaps he once was one of those Latter-Day Saints or Mormons who settled in the Great Salt Lake area."

"This man was no saint, not by anyone's definition! I thought sure he was going to rape me then and there!"

"Perhaps he was once a good Mormon, but his behavior got him into trouble with the religious authorities. I understand that those Mormon church leaders hold their members to a strict code of behavior, and if the member sins too egregiously he can be banished or shunned."

"Well, I can imagine something like that happened with this man! We will never catch him and bring him to justice, will we?"

"No, I don't think we will. But there will be justice in the end!"

Grace was silent for a few seconds and then said, "Mr. Chouteau, you impress me as an educated man and as a Christian. But it seems odd to me that you would take a job with this wagon train as a scout. I realize this might be impolite of me to ask, but why aren't you back in the civilized part of the country, like Saint Louis, pursuing a career commensurate with your education? You must have some special reason you are so far from home."

"Miss Clark, you have surmised correctly that I am an educated man and a Christian. I was educated by the Jesuits at Saint Louis College, and I have accompanied Fr. De Smet, whom you may have heard of, on some of his missionary trips to the western tribes. I served as a translator. And so, you might say I have put my education as a linguist and as a lay student of the Catholic faith to good use."

"Yes, indeed so sir! But that does not explain your presence on this cross-country trek. You also impress me as a man of sorrows, acquainted with grief. Is there something that has driven you away from your home? Oh, forgive me for being so inquisitive and prying into your private affairs, but it seems to me that you could use someone to share your grief."

Blue Feather gave a sad smile and was silent for a few moments. Then he said, "I didn't want to burden anyone with my troubles, Miss Clark. Especially you since you have your own losses to grieve. But I will tell you my story if you so desire. You could be shocked by these events that I will relate, but I have confessed my sins. I just haven't experienced any release from my shame and guilt."

"You can tell me your story Mr. Chouteau, and I will not judge you. I only want to help you, as you have been helping me."

Blue Feather looked into her eyes and could see her sincerity, and so he told her his story starting with his first love Winnie and then his relationship with Louise Marie. He left nothing out.

When he finished his story, he was silent, and looked down at his boots. Grace Clark sighed and after a few seconds said,

"Mr. Chouteau, I can see now that you attempted to run away from your grief and shame. You are grieving for your precious wife Winnie and at the same time feeling great shame and guilt over being unfaithful to Winnie with Louise Marie. Tell me Mr. Chouteau, do you love Louise Marie? And does she love you? Will she be kind and faithful to you, and can you be the same to her?"

"To answer your questions, yes! But I don't think that I love her as much as I loved Winnie."

"Mr. Chouteau, you have a long history with Winnie and the two of you had many years to grow in your love for each other. You had known Louise Marie for only a few days before you married her, and only for a few weeks on your trek back to Missouri. You must allow your love to grow, and it will grow in time if you practice it."

"Practice it?"

"Yes, mindfully behave in a loving manner with her. She will respond in kind even if she does not immediately behave in that manner with you."

"Well, thank you Miss Clark. Talking did indeed help. I only wish I could do more for you. Perhaps my prayers for your comfort and healing will have to suffice."

"Thank you for your prayers, Mr. Chouteau! And I will pray for you!"

♋   ♋   ♋

The wagon train continued its northwesterly trek covering about three miles per hour. On the second day of their resumed trek Blue Feather spotted a rider slumped over on his saddle obviously in a hard way. He was wearing nothing but his white, long underwear or "undergarment" as the Latter-Day Saints called them. Blue Feather rode to intercept him.

Pulling alongside him and grabbing the rider's reins, Blue Feather said, "Whoa! Hold on fellow...let's see what has happened to you."

The rider's eyes had been mostly closed, but they opened when he realized Blue Feather's presence. "I was beat up and robbed of my horses and buckskins by the Shoshone! Gol darn it, they took my guns as well!"

"You are fortunate that they didn't kill you outright! I'm going to take you to our doctor, and then after he treats you, we'll see about some clothes you can borrow."

Returning to the wagon train towing the underclad rider behind him, Blue Feather sought out the doctor. The doctor pulled over in his wagon and examined the young man who appeared to be in his mid-20s. He had reddish blond hair and beard and blue eyes and stood about six feet tall. The thought crossed his mind that this could have been the phony Indian who had attacked Grace Clark.

With that in mind, late that afternoon Blue Feather asked five young men in the wagon company to stop by the doctor's tent. Unbeknownst to them, Grace was inspecting them through a peephole, having been asked to identify the man who had accosted her while dressed as an Indian.

When all six men had been carefully examined, Grace was asked by Blue Feather, "Did any of these men look like the man who accosted you?"

Grace answered, "Well, no. None of them looked like the man who accosted me. But the man with the reddish beard and blue eyes looked familiar. He could have been in that raiding party and he might know who the tall man is!"

"I must interrogate this man and see if he knows who murdered your mother and brother, and who accosted you!" said Blue Feather.

Johannes ran up to Blue Feather and said, "That man who was calling himself Harald Olsen, just stole a horse and galloped out of here!"

"Did you see which way he went?"

"Yeah, that way," he said pointing in a southeasterly direction.

Blue Feather ran for his horse. He already had his weapons, but Captain Gregg held up his hand and said, "Whoa! Where are you going?"

"The young man we rescued has stolen a horse and escaped! He is the only person who can identify the men who shot and killed the Clarks and accosted Grace!"

"Blue Feather, you haven't thought this out! What are you going to do if you catch him? We don't have a cell to put him in, and there are no officers of the law that can arrest him or the men he identifies. I hate to take the wind out of your sails, but this would be a fool's errand! Not to mention, you are still needed as a scout for this wagon train."

"Well, you are my employer as well as my friend, and I can see now that I kind of flew off the handle. It just that I hate to see injustices like the murders of the Clarks go unpunished."

"And I suppose you are like the other young men on this wagon train who have taken to the lovely young Miss Grace Clark and want to help her."

"What! No, I have no special interest in Miss Clark. Besides, I am married again!"

"Married again?! I didn't know you were previously married."

"Oh, it's a long story. But my first wife, Winnie, died in the cholera epidemic in St. Louis. Just recently I met a young woman from Saint Charles and married her. There's a lot more to the story, but I don't want to go into it right now."

CHAPTER SIXTEEN

Some days later the wagon train reached Fort Hall where they intended to stop and rest the livestock and buy provisions for the rest of the trek. As they pulled in, Blue Feather noticed a regiment of dragoons led by two lieutenants. Blue Feather would find out later their names were Nathaniel Lyon and J.W. Davison.

Captain Greg was riding next to Blue Feather when the dragoons came into view. Captain Gregg said, "Blue Feather, let's go pay our respects to those cavalry officers there. You never know when you might need a friend in the U.S. Army in our line of work!"

"Greetings, Lieutenants! I am Jedediah Gregg leader of this here wagon train bound for Oregon, and this is Blue Feather Chouteau, my scout."

"We are Lieutenants Nathaniel Lyon and J.W. Davison, and we are leading this regiment of dragoons to California. We are planning to continue on the Oregon Trail and then turn south into California. We will be leaving in two days at first light. If you like, we can leave together, and we will provide an Army escort."

"That sounds like an excellent idea, thank you Lieutenant Lyon."

On the morning of their departure Lieutenant Lyon rode up to Captain Gregg and said, "I will lead a column of soldiers in front of the wagon train and Lieutenant Davison will lead a column following the wagon train. There have been some attacks by renegade Indians recently and your people will be protected both front and back."

"Thanks again, Lieutenant. We are ready to get going when you say the word."

"We are glad to be of service, Mr. Gregg. Say, I noticed that you have a half-breed scout. Could you ask him to ride next to me for a spell today? I'm curious to hear what he says about the Indian tribes in these parts."

"That should not be a problem, Lieutenant. But sir, I urge you to show respect to Blue Feather. He is an educated man and a protégé of the great Father Pierre-Jean De Smet."

"That is good to know. I will keep that in mind," said Lt. Lyon. But in his mind, he thought, *why bother to educate these savages? In an ideal world they would be removed to some desolate rural areas and taught to farm. They need nothing more than training on the simple tasks of running a farm.*

In the days that passed, the lieutenants grew more appreciative of Blue Feather's skills as a scout. On two different occasions he had alerted the soldiers and wagon train of an ambush by rogue Indians. In the second skirmish the Army captured a wounded warrior who spoke some English. They discovered that he belonged to the Etch-ka-taw-wah Indians who lived along the Applegate River in southwestern Oregon.

Blue Feather requested that the wagon train surgeon be allowed to treat the injured warrior, who was little more than a boy at 16 years.

"Lieutenants, it will work to our favor if we get our physician to treat this young brave. It would be a gesture of peace."

The lieutenants exchanged glances when Blue Feather came to them with his request.

"Blue Feather, if we bind up this boy's wounds what is to stop him from attacking us again? And what if he tells his compadres that we are cowards and fearful of further attacks? We don't want to appear weak before our enemy."

"Treating the young warrior is a goodwill gesture. We can't expect to make peace with any Indian tribe if all we do is kill them! Of course, we must fight back if they attack us. But if we don't deal with them humanely, they have no reason to stop treating us like the enemy."

In the end, Blue Feather was allowed to fetch the wagon train's physician. Fortunately, the young warrior's wounds did not involve any vital organs, and after a week of convalescence he was well-enough to return to his people. But Lt. Lyon noted that Blue Feather was too tender-hearted for some of the actions he wanted to take against the California Indians that this army regiment had been sent to subdue and control.

Blue Feather introduced himself to Soaring Falcon, the 16-year-old brave who was convalescing.

"I am Blue Feather, of the Osage tribe in Missouri."

"Where is this place Missouri?"

"If you were to follow the great river to the southeast you would eventually enter Missouri. This would be a trip of many days."

"Why do you help these white people to move here and take our land? Is there not enough land to the east? Oh, now I see, you are half white and have no loyalty to your Indian parent."

"Soaring Falcon, that is not true. I honor both my French father and my Osage mother, but my first loyalty is to God in heaven. God loves all his people, white, red, black, brown, and yellow; and He wants all of His children to love one another and live peaceably together."

"Live peaceably together? You are a dreamer, Blue Feather. My people are sworn to drive out the white devils who steal our land and kill us. There will be no peace until you are all dead!"

"Soaring Falcon, let me tell you about my God and His peace that surpasses understanding."

"Stop! I don't want to hear about your white man's god. If he were a god of peace, would he allow your white brothers to kill us Indians? No, you speak of nonsense. Leave me now!"

At this point Blue Feather decided to quit trying to reach out to the young warrior. He felt he had failed but then recalled his experience as a youngster with his classmate at the Jesuit school for Indian boys. People must come to faith on their own accord and this young brave was not ready to listen.

The next day Soaring Falcon mounted his pony, which had been found and kept on a tether, and rode off in search of his tribe.

Some days later the travelers encountered another raiding party of about twelve warriors from the Etch-ka-taw-wah tribe. The combined forces of the soldiers and armed settlers were too much for the warriors. Seven warriors were killed, but only one of the soldiers and settlers was killed. After the battle Lt. Lyon found the body of his scout with three arrows in it. Among the dead Indians was Soaring Falcon.

"Those red savages killed our scout, leaving him looking like his mother's pin cushion. Well, I suppose it falls on me to write his family that their son and husband died bravely in battle, and so forth."

"It is our solemn duty," Lt. Davison said.

"Solemnity is not my strong suit! Davison, you believe in God -- you are much better suited to this sort of thing. You should write the letter."

"In the meantime, I want to tell Blue Feather that his effort to reach out in peace to the Etch-ka-taw-wah tribe was a foolish thing to do."

Two days later Captain Gregg and his wagon train arrived at Oregon City, their final destination.

At the evening meal at the captain's campfire, Captain Gregg discussed his plans with Blue Feather. "Well, my friend, this is the end of the line for these settlers. I, myself am tempted to plant roots here. I haven't decided yet, but I will spend at least a week resting here. The De Jong family is making noises about staying here as well. They have been with me for several years but now they're feeling like settling down themselves. What about you, Blue Feather?"

"I must return to Missouri to my wife. I have responsibilities."

"Well, yes, of course. I will pay you now for your services, and I am including a bonus out of appreciation for all that you have done so excellently."

At this point Lieutenants Lyon and Davison walked up to the campfire. "Blue Feather Choteau, we would appreciate a word with you now, if you don't mind."

Blue Feather looked at his friend, Captain Gregg who gestured that he should go ahead.

Blue Feather walked with the Lieutenants toward the army encampment. Lt. Lyon started the conversation, "Blue Feather, as you know, this regiment needs to replace its scout. Our mission is to continue south to Fort Orford on the coast, and then after replenishing our provisions, to travel into California and pacify the Pomo Indians who have been murdering white settlers."

Lt. Davison, jumped in, "We know about your past service with the U.S. Army as a scout and that you held the rank of warrant officer. We can reinstate you in the Army for a fixed period of service, not to exceed 90 days."

Blue Feather was thinking of how the money would come in handy and said "I want to prayerfully consider your offer. Can I give you my answer in the morning?"

"Yes, we'll be departing for Fort Orford the day after tomorrow."

♋ ♋ ♋

Blue Feather decided to join the army regiment. Several days into their journey after their stop at Fort Orford, the regiment of dragoons came to a point where a stream of fresh footprints indicating several persons had marched from the south to the west, i.e., in the direction of the coast. The path appeared to lead to a break in the coastal range of relatively low mountains. Together these signs appeared to indicate to Blue Feather that a large group of hunters and gatherers left from a village south of their location to go to the coast to fish or possibly to hunt animals such as seals. Blue Feather explained his thoughts to the lieutenants. Conferring between themselves the lieutenants decided to divide the regiment into two companies, one continuing south under the leadership of Lt. Lyon, and the second heading west under the leadership of Lt. Davison. Blue Feather would track the group of hunters and gatherers on the westward trek. It would be clear to anyone observing the interaction of the two officers that this division was Lt. Lyon's idea and he insisted on his way.

☙ ☙ ☙

Lt. Lyon was giving orders to his first sergeant, "The Pomo village is located on a small island in Clearwater Lake. Under the cover of darkness tonight, I want you to determine if the island can be reached by our horses or if the water is too deep."

With a sharp salute the first sergeant said, "Yes sir!"

That night arriving at the lake, the first sergeant quickly decided that the lake was too deep for the horses to ford. But looking down the lakeshore, he was happy to find several canoes pulled up on the ground.

"Corporal, report to the lieutenant that the lake is too deep to ford, but we found seven canoes we can use to reach the island."

Lt. Lyon was delighted to hear this news and immediately ordered his troops forward to the lake, keeping as quiet as possible.

When they arrived at the lake they dismounted and tethered their horses to trees and waited for the deepest part of the night according to the lieutenant's orders. At approximately 11 PM Lt. Lyon called his men to order and told them his orders, "Men, we are here to avenge the deaths of multiple white settlers who were killed by the Pomo Indians. We have been ordered to eradicate this village. We are ordered to kill every last man, woman, and child, just as God Himself commanded the Hebrews to wipe out all the Canaanite tribes, so that the land would be theirs."

Some of the soldiers were quietly disturbed by the order to kill women and children. Men exchanged glances with their closest comrades in arms and with a slight movement of the head or lips, they indicated that they didn't plan to follow orders. They could always fire their rifles and intentionally miss, and no one would be the wiser. But others among the troops wanted to go on a killing spree. These men didn't distinguish between the Pomo and the Comanche, Cheyenne, Kiowa, or Apache, and they would gladly kill any Indian to avenge their friends lost in previous battles with hostile tribes.

Sneaking across the lake to the island in the borrowed canoes, the soldiers collected on the shore and Lt. Lyon waited until all of his men were present. Then he issued the order: they were to go through the village and shoot into the homes of the Pomo while they slept. But when the shooting started, many of the villagers awoke and streamed out their huts. These people were quickly shot down. The soldiers did not encounter any resistance.

♋ ♋ ♋

Meanwhile, Lt. Davison and his company, following Blue Feather's tracking, caught up to the campground of the hunters who had left the village to kill game and bring back meat to their families. It was night and the Pomo hunters were asleep. Lt. Davison ordered his men to execute a pincer movement to flank the campground. One man on the right and one man on the left were ordered to fire their weapons into the sky to announce their arrival.

The noise woke the Pomo and they jumped up in chaos and confusion. Their leader, whom later they would learn was Chief Augustine, spoke to his braves in their native language telling them not to resist. He then spoke in Spanish to Lt. Davison, "We are not here to fight, just to hunt, and bring meat back to our families in the village. We are not raiders! You can see that we have only two burros with us to carry the meat back to the village."

Lt. Davison turned to his men and asked, "Does anyone know what this savage has said?"

Blue Feather said, "I understand him. He is speaking Spanish. He just said that they are simply on a hunting trip to feed their families. They are not warriors. Warriors would be riding horses and they only have donkeys to carry the meat back to the village."

"Tell him that his men are under arrest for the murder of Andrew Kelsey and Charles Stone and that they will be tried as criminals."

After Blue Feather translated this for the Pomo leader he said,

"You do not know the truth! These two men, Kelsey and Stone had made slaves of us! They forced us to work as vaqueros and to mine for gold. They locked us in a stockade and did not provide enough rations to survive. Some of us starved. And worst of all, they took our wives and daughters and raped them and threatened to kill them if we did not give them up!"

Lt. Davison stirred uneasily in his saddle, sweat pouring down his face even though the night was cool. He turned to Blue Feather, "Do you think this man is telling the truth?"

Blue Feather said, "Let me find out more about this man." Speaking in Spanish, Blue Feather asked, "What is your name? Are you the chief of the Pomos?"

"My name is Augustine. I am the chief of the Pomos."

"You are named after Saint Augustine. Are you a Christian?"

"Yes, we are all baptized Catholics. Our nation has been Catholic ever since the Spanish arrived generations ago. And that reminds me of another evil these two men committed against us. They drove out our priests and we have not had the sacraments since then."

Blue Feather translated the chief's response for Lt. Davison and then added, "Lieutenant, the Pomo nation impresses me as a peaceful Christian tribe who had been enslaved by the two white settlers. The Pomos had suffered greatly under their abuse until finally they resorted to violence to free themselves."

Lt. Davison nervously wiped his brow with a handkerchief and said, "Blue Feather, can you find your way to the Pomo village and report to Lt. Lyon what we heard here, and ask him what he wants us to do regarding the arrest of these people? I'll wait here with my soldiers until we hear from you."

Blue Feather nodded yes and wheeled his horse around to head off to the Pomo village. Fortunately, there was a full moon and there was just enough light to find his way back to the trail that led to the Pomo village.

As he approached the village, he realized that it was located on a small island in the middle of a lake. He tied up his horse with those belonging to the soldiers and found a canoe to carry him to the island. As he stepped ashore, he noticed that there appeared to be people lying about on the ground just outside of their crude dwellings. They did not stir, nor look up. The soldiers in Lt. Lyon's company were huddled into two groups. Soldiers in one group were loud and jovial, boasting about what they had done. Soldiers in the other group only whispered among themselves. Blue Feather noticed their grief-stricken faces and, in some cases, tears welling up in their eyes.

Blue Feather walked up to Sergeant Preston Forrest, whom he had befriended on their trek. "Sergeant Forrest, what happened here? Why are these people lying on the ground as if they were... dead?"

Then to answer his own question, he continued walking into the village and noticed that these were the dead bodies of 112 Indians, mostly women and children, and only a handful of old men. It took several seconds to process what he was seeing – he was shocked beyond words, beyond thought even. Then an overwhelming wave of grief hit him, and he fell to his knees. Blue Feather thought to pray but he could not formulate his thoughts; bewildered, he fell face down.

Sergeant Forrest came up and put a hand on Blue Feather's shoulder, "Let me tell you how this happened. Lt. Lyon ordered us to kill every man, woman, and child. He made an analogy to Moses in Exodus who was commanded by God to kill all the nations native to the land of Canaan. I thought this was odd because he is generally antagonistic to religion. I think he might have simply wanted to justify this genocidal act."

"Did every soldier participate in the killing?"

"No, the soldiers you see in this group fired their weapons but intentionally missed. None of us shot anyone. We made a good show of it, that's all."

"Did any Pomo escape?"

"Yes, perhaps sixty or so women and children."

"We caught up with the hunters from this village who claimed only two white men were killed, men who had enslaved them, held back rations and starved some of them, and took their daughters as sex slaves. I must report this to the commanding officer at Fort Orford."

"Oh, my Lord! This is far worse than I thought. Yes, the authorities must hear your telling of the incident. But before you leave let me finish my written testimony, which I will sign, and twenty-five more of us will sign."

"OK, right now I want to find Lt. Lyon."

"A moment ago, I saw him headed to the latrine," the Sergeant pointed out the direction.

"Perfect!"

Blue Feather ran to the latrine and as he arrived, Lt. Lyon was just finishing his business.

"Ah, Mr. Chouteau, you have returned! Well, you missed all the excitement here! The island became a perfect slaughtering pen!"

Blue Feather felt a rage he had never felt before and struck Lt. Lyon with a fierce blow to the nose. While he was still reeling backward, Blue Feather struck him again hard in the stomach and then an uppercut to the jaw. The lieutenant fell backward into the latrine.

"I'll see that you are court-martialed for this!"

"That won't happen because I will tell the authorities what you did here! The large-scale murder of women, children, and the elderly. You are a disgrace to the uniform!"

Still in his prone position, Lt. Lyon raised his pistol to shoot Blue Feather, but Blue Feather kicked the weapon out of his hand further into the muck.

"You have done more than enough killing tonight!"

Blue Feather quickly returned to his horse and began galloping in the direction of the hunters' camp. When he arrived, he found Lt. Davison who asked, "What are Lt. Lyon's orders?"

Without hesitation Blue Feather said "Lyon said to release them. We have insufficient evidence to support an arrest."

Lt. Davison looked a little confused, but shook it off and said,

"Well, I think under the circumstances that is the best course of action."

Blue Feather rode on to Fort Orford and upon arrival went directly to the Command section. When he heard that the matter involved Lt. Lyon and genocide, the colonel's aide, a captain named O'Connor, showed Blue Feather into the colonel's office. The colonel looked at Blue Feather and said, "Who are you and what is this about?"

"I am Blue Feather Chouteau and until recently I was serving as a scout and tracker for Lieutenants Lyon and Davison in their mission to pacify the Pomo and bring the murderers of two white settlers to justice."

"Well, was the mission accomplished? And why aren't the lieutenants making this report?"

"Sir, the mission was not accomplished. The Army was lied to -- this wasn't a group of hostile Indians killing innocent white settlers. Far be that from the truth! The two settlers who had been killed had enslaved the Pomo nation, locking them up in a stockade, starving them with insufficient rations, using them as forced labor, and taking Pomo wives and daughters from families to use for their sexual amusement. When the Pomo could stand it no longer and the opportunity arose, they killed their captors. Lt. Lyon did nothing to investigate the situation. His mind was made up that these Pomo were hostiles and should be eliminated. He and his men killed 112 women, children, and elderly Pomo Indians. The young men were on a hunting trip and not present for this act of genocide."

"These are serious charges you are making! And I'm sure that Lt. Lyon will present an entirely different story. Without any witnesses, it's just your word against Lt. Lyon's word. And I know whom the Army will decide to believe."

"Colonel, there are witnesses. Twenty-six of them, in fact. This paper I'm handing you is from Sergeant Forrest. He wrote out his testimony and had the signatures of twenty-five enlisted men on the back of his written testimony."

"Lt. Davison was not present?"

"No sir. The regiment had divided into two companies. One was to locate the village and the second, which Lt. Davison commanded, was to locate the hunting party composed of the young men of the village."

"So, you were not a witness to the alleged genocide?"

"No sir, I was with Lt. Davison."

"Then all you have provided is just hearsay."

"Sir, you have written testimony of Sergeant Preston Forrest about the incident and signatures of 25 enlisted men affirming his statement. And sir, I have written down my testimony about my conversation with Chief Augustine who described what the two white settlers did to the Pomo which led to the rebellion."

"And you believe what this chief told you, without verification?"

"Well, sir, I think that further investigation would be the responsibility of Army officers, not a temporary soldier such as myself."

"Hmmpf! You are dismissed Mr. Blue Feather. Collect your pay at the paymaster," the colonel said handing him a note authorizing his payment. "Then go back to wherever you came from. Your services are no longer needed."

Blue Feather collected his pay and bought some provisions for the trip home to Missouri. He didn't waste any time leaving and he didn't look back.

CHAPTER SEVENTEEN

Blue Feather returned to Missouri riding alone for the 2,000 miles of the Oregon Trail. He stopped at the Army forts along the way like the wagon train he had served heading west. Other than the occasional wagon train heading west, he saw no other living souls on his journey, neither Indian nor white settler. The solitude proved to be good for Blue Feather, giving him time to pray and soul-search. But the nights were haunted with ghosts. Sometimes he would dream of Winnie, only to wake up and remember his terrible loss again. Other times he would dream of Louise Marie, which was pleasant at the time but then he would awake and wonder if he had made the right decision to marry her after knowing her only a matter of days. Of course, his friends Shamus and White Fawn were happily married and had decided to marry within hours of meeting each other. He thought perhaps things would work out for him after all. But he continued to be plagued with doubts.

Blue Feather did not encounter many people, white settlers or Indians, on his trek homeward, but that did not mean he was alone. At night, he would he hear the stirrings of large animals near his camp. He kept his campfire going as long as he could. That would not keep of the predators at bay, but at least if he were awakened by an animal, he might be able to see it by the firelight.

One night he awoke to the frightened cries of his horse who had caught the scent of a cougar lurking about. Blue Feather picked up his six gun which he kept by his side and sat up. He heard the cries of the cougar and then growling and barking of a large dog. He could not see this happening, but he sensed that the large dog had scared off the cougar. But then a remarkable thing happened. The large dog trotted back to the camp and curled up next to Blue Feather. When he awoke at dawn Blue Feather was astonished to see that Grigio, the gray wolf dog that had appointed himself protector of Fr. De Smet, had found him.

"Grigio, it's so good to see you after all these years! But how is this possible? You don't seem to have aged any in all this time, and where did you come from?" Of course, the dog did not answer him, but he did seem to smile at Blue Feather.

Grigio chose to accompany Blue Feather on his solitary return to Missouri. The dog's mission was clear – protect Blue Feather from any harm from animal or human. Toward the end of their journey in northern Kansas Blue Feather awoke from his slumber one night when Grigio jumped up and barked at intruders into their camp -- a raiding party of Sioux warriors. One warrior was trying to lead away Blue Feather's fine chestnut stallion, but the horse was not cooperating. Blue Feather sat up and grabbed his six-shooter saying (in Sioux), "It seems that my horse does not want to go with you! I suggest that you leave him where you found him."

"Ha! The half-breed speaks our tongue! Well, that doesn't change your situation any. There are ten of us and only one of you. You can't stop us!"

"Oh, but you are overlooking my companion. It upsets him greatly when he thinks someone or something might try to hurt me or steal from me."

Then without warning Grigio leaped up to the rider attempting to steal Blue Feather's stallion, grabbing his wrist with his powerful jaws and pulling him off his palomino. In response, two warriors tried to shoot the dog with their arrows. But Grigio easily dodged them, prompting the leader of the raiding party to say, "This is a demon dog! I heard a story of such a demon protecting a black robe – the white man's shaman."

"I am giving you fair warning. This is no ordinary dog. No, this dog is powerful medicine sent by my God to protect me. It would be best for you to get away while you still can!"

The Sioux warriors had witnessed enough and hastily withdrew from Blue Feather and his dog's powerful medicine.

When his would-be attackers fled out of sight Blue Feather spoke to Grigio, "I hope I didn't misspeak when I said that you had been sent by God to protect me."

In response, Grigio happily trotted over to Blue Feather's side and leaned into him as large dogs sometimes do to express their liking for you. Then Blue Feather had the distinct impression that the big dog was smiling as he hugged and petted him.

♋   ♋   ♋

Blue Feather's trek was nearly complete when he made camp the next day. As had become his habit, Blue Feather spoke to Grigio as if he were a sentient being, "Well, tomorrow my friend we will cross the Missouri River and enter my home state. Then we will be home in just a few days of riding. I can hardly wait now to see Louise Marie. I have wronged her terribly by running away from my responsibilities to her – I hope she can forgive me."

For his part Grigio looked at Blue Feather as he spoke, turning his head sideways as dogs sometimes do when it seems that they are listening carefully to you.

After building a campfire, Blue Feather cooked a dinner of sorts. He noticed that Grigio never ate any food that he cooked. Blue Feather thought that this was a bit curious but figured that the dog was finding his own food such as squirrels and prairie dogs and that his refusal to eat Blue Feather's fare was not intended as an affront. After setting out his bedroll, Blue Feather and his companion settled down for a night's sleep.

The next morning Blue Feather thought he felt a lick or kiss on his cheek, and he woke up. But Grigio was nowhere to be seen. He called for the dog a few times as he ate breakfast and fed and watered his horse, but Grigio did not respond. Blue Feather experienced a sense of loss in his heart but figured that perhaps it was time for his God-appointed guardian to move on. After all, he no longer was in the wilderness but instead in the well-settled farmland of eastern Kansas.

A few days later Blue Feather and his fine chestnut stallion loped onto his farm. He could see that Louise Marie had planted flowers in front of the white farmhouse, making it a more inviting place. When he was still 200 feet from the hitching post in front of his home, a young woman stepped out of the house onto the porch and sat down on the steps. She was carrying a baby girl! As he drew closer the woman practically jumped up and excitedly walked over as he dismounted. It was Louise Marie, and she was obviously the baby's mother!

"Blue Feather! At last, you have returned! So much has happened this past year while you were away. Meet your daughter – her name is Christine!"

Blue Feather had some difficulty finding his voice, "I have a daughter?"

"Yes, did I not just tell you that?" Louise Marie said with a smile.

"Oh my gosh, I want to hold and kiss both of you!"

"Oh no you don't! Not until you wash up and get out of those filthy trail clothes!"

Blue Feather could see that there was no choice but to comply, so he walked his horse over to the corral holding his farm mules and took off his saddle. Then he spotted a new building on the farm. He caught his wife's attention and asked, "What is this?"

"That is a wash house that Shamus built for us. You go in there and start bathing yourself, *thoroughly with soap!*" she said with emphasis, as if talking to a little boy. "I'll bring some clean clothes for you."

All washed and in clean clothes for the first time in months Blue Feather felt like he had been reborn. *Well, perhaps I have been reborn, because I am starting a new life as a husband and father!*

The reunion was sweet with Blue Feather first hugging the mother and their child and kissing her passionately, and then holding his daughter laughing and kissing her little cheeks. Christine looked up and smiled at her father and Blue Feather's heart just melted.

"Oh, I am so sorry that I left you. That was thoughtless leaving you behind all alone!"

"I was never alone, White Fawn and her husband were here frequently, and I was often at their place sharing a meal. White Fawn was a most skillful midwife and taught me how to care for a newborn baby. Then there was my constant guardian, Emmanuelle. I gave her that name because it means God with us."

"Where is Emmanuelle now? Does she live on a nearby farm?"

"Emmanuelle is the name I gave her. She is a large white wolf dog, a beautiful specimen, who just showed up one day. I found her resting on the porch and that is where she slept. I didn't even feed her. She didn't want to eat from my table. I figured she was hunting her own food. You know, rabbits and squirrels."

"Where is she now?"

"I don't know. I haven't seen her for days now. Maybe she felt it was time to move on."

Blue Feather sat down heavily on the front steps. "Oh my gosh!" he said staring into space.

"Is there something wrong?" Louise Marie said with a worried expression.

"No, everything is fine. It's just that...Well, I have to tell you about Grigio."

Louise Marie listened with amazement at Blue Feather's story. Then they looked at each other, and Blue Feather said, "The Bible says that we should not neglect to entertain strangers because they might turn out to be angels. I guess that applies to strange dogs who come to rescue and protect us."

"Furry angels? Who would have ever expected this?"

♋   ♋   ♋

Some weeks later Blue Feather and Louise Marie exchanged vows in a Catholic ceremony conducted by Fr. De Smet. Afterwards, Shamus and White Fawn held a reception for the newlyweds in their home.

Fr. De Smet asked Blue Feather what he would do now that he was a father. Without hesitation Blue Feather replied, "I will farm this land, being content with what we produce and sell, love my wife, and love and raise my child. This is the important work the Lord has set before me."

"Well said, my son! Your words mirror what St. John Chrysostom said in 400 AD:

Have no concern for money. Love your wife more than you love your own life. Never be at odds but be true. Prefer her company at home above being out. Esteem and admire her publicly and advise her patiently. Pray together, go to church, and discuss the readings and Prayers. If your marriage is like this, your perfection will rival the holiest of monks."

"I will follow these words of wisdom, I promise Fr. De Smet."

"And I will help him keep his promise!" said Louise Marie, smiling and joining her husband.

AFTERWORD

Historical Figures in this Story

This is a work of fiction, but it was woven around historical events, and in some cases, historical figures. It is important not to interpret the events described in this story as history, but rather as historical fiction. That said, there are some strong similarities between the real events and the stories told in this book.

Thomas Clark and Family: This family emigrated from England and was surprisingly adventurous. The family was composed of the mother and siblings of Thomas Clark. Thomas traveled with his mother, his 25-year-old sister Grace, his 17-year-old brother, Hodgson, another brother named Charlie, and another married sister with her family. He had a comfortable carriage custom built for Grace to drive and his mother to ride in, perhaps the first to cross the plains. The survivors of the Shoshone attack went on to become successful citizens of Oregon. Grace Clark married Thomas' business partner, Jackson Vandevert, and settled in the Willamette Valley, raising seven children. Despite her tragic early encounter with the Shoshone, Grace worked tirelessly for the well-being of the local Native Americans in Oregon.

Father Pierre Jean De Smet (1801-1873): Jan De Smet, born and raised in Belgium, was a Catholic priest and member of the Society of Jesus (Jesuits). He was well known for his extensive missionary work among Native Americans in the midwestern and northwestern United States and western Canada during the mid-19th century. His missionary journeys totaled about 180,000 miles

In 1820 De Smet enrolled at the Petit Séminaire at Mechelen, then emigrated to the United States in 1821 with eleven other Belgian Jesuits, each with hopes of becoming a missionary to Native Americans. He began studying for the priesthood in Maryland, then in 1823, De Smet moved to the Jesuit seminary in Florissant, Missouri, northwest of St. Louis, to complete his theological studies. He also began his studies of Indian languages. In 1827 he was ordained a priest.

He became known and respected as the "Friend of Sitting Bull", because he convinced the Sioux war chief to partake in negotiations with the federal government for the 1868 Treaty of Fort Laramie.

Grigio: I borrowed Grigio the protective dog from Catholic lore about St. John Bosco, an Italian priest who was famous for working with impoverished youth who otherwise might become criminals. This work sometimes took John into dangerous neighborhoods. Don Bosco was crossing Turin one night in 1852 through the Valdocco, a dangerous part of the city. He was careful as he had been attacked previously in this neighborhood. Suddenly a large, gray dog ran right up to him. At first, the good priest was startled, but after the dog showed signs of friendliness, he allowed him to walk with him. When they approached the gate of his home, the dog trotted away. This happened every time he had to walk home late at night. Over the course of decades, the dog appeared on several occasions to protect Don Bosco. On one occasion, it somehow left the house where John Don Bosco was staying, when all the doors and windows were locked shut. The priest named the dog Grigio, (GREE-jo), "the grey one." Was

Grigio truly a historical figure? We probably won't know in this life.

Colonel Kearney: This fellow was a composite of two historic military leaders of the same family. These were Philip Kearny Jr. (June 1, 1815 – September 1, 1862), and his uncle Stephen Watts Kearny (sometimes spelled Kearney) (August 30, 1794 – October 31, 1848). They came from a wealthy New York family. They were both highly accomplished Army officers.

Other historical figures:
Chief Augustine of the Pomo Nation
Lt. John Wynn Davidson (August 14, 1825 – June 26, 1881)
General Nathaniel Lyon (1818 - 1861)
John Mullanphy (1758 – 1833)
Andrew Kelsey and Charles Stone
Chief Sauganash

www.ingramcontent.com/pod-product-compliance
Lightning Source LLC
Chambersburg PA
CBHW031340170626
46807CB00002B/776